"I don't want you to go."

The pleas tugged at him, made him think about doing stupid things that didn't fit with his life or the need to keep her protected. "You'll be safe with him."

Her other hand went to his lap. Smoothed up and down his thigh. "You make me feel safe."

The touching, the sound of her voice, the pleading in those big eyes. He was ten seconds from breaking. "Don't do this."

She nuzzled her mouth against his neck. Blew a warm breath over his skin. He fought it until he couldn't, then he turned his head and kissed her. Right there in another man's house, in a place with security but no connection to Cam.

It took every ounce of his strength and self-control to pull back. When that didn't give him enough space, he stood up. Paced around and thought about airplanes. Anything to take his mind off her face and the touch of those lips.

"Then I'm going with you."

CORNERED

HelenKay Dimon

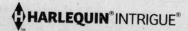

For all the readers who asked for more Corcoran Team books—
thank you! I love these guys, too.

Recycling programs
for this product may
not exist in your area.

ISBN-13: 978-0-373-69838-7

Cornered

Copyright © 2015 by HelenKay Dimon

Printed in U.S.A.

www.Harlequin.com

HelenKay Dimon, an award-winning author, spent twelve years in the most unromantic career ever—divorce lawyer. After dedicating all that effort to helping people terminate relationships, she is thrilled to deal in happy endings and write romance novels for a living. Now her days are filled with gardening, writing, reading and spending time with her family in and around San Diego. Stop by her website, helenkaydimon.com, and say hello.

Books by HelenKay Dimon

HARLEQUIN INTRIGUE

Corcoran Team: Bulletproof Bachelors series

Cornered

Corcoran Team series

Fearless
Ruthless
Relentless
Lawless
Traceless

Mystery Men series

Under the Gun
Guns and the Girl Next Door
Gunning for Trouble
Locked and Loaded
The Big Guns

Visit the Author Profile page at Harlequin.com for more titles.

CAST OF CHARACTERS

Cameron Roth—Former Navy pilot turned Corcoran Team member. He's a confirmed bachelor looking to stay focused on work and rescuing. When a simple assignment turns upside down, he drags a woman along on his mission. He thinks she's an innocent bystander, but when it becomes clear she's intimately tied to the secrets unfolding around him, he ends up protecting her...and more.

Julia White—Julia didn't so much leave Calapan Island as she escaped it. She is ready to leave her past behind and makes one last trip to her old hometown to tie up loose ends. She's in the wrong place at the wrong time when Cam crashes into her life—literally—and lands in danger.

Ray Miner—He is the mysterious man with an agenda and a lot of muscle on his side. He's used fake identities, ordered an attack on Julia and tried to kill Cam. There's no question he's on Calapan to cause trouble.

Bud Kreider—The police chief on Calapan. He possesses a good-old-boy vibe and doesn't want the Corcoran Team on his turf. He also seems to be one step behind and confused about what's happening on the island.

Sandy Bartlet—An old friend of Julia's father. He's a mainstay on Calapan. He's lived there and made his fortune. Now he's retired and trying to give back to his community. When Julia and Cam need help, Sandy is the man they run to.

Holt Kingston—The leader of the Corcoran's traveling team. He trusts his men and comes to Calapan to support Cam. He's not a guy who trusts easily and he can't find anyone on Calapan worth trusting.

Chapter One

A crack of gunfire echoed through the towering trees. That sort of thing would have sent Julia White scrambling for her cell phone and dialing for the police back in her normal life. But not on Calapan Island, the tiny strip of land miles from Seattle and accessible only by ferry. Here people fired weapons for sport, as a warning or just because it was Tuesday.

She didn't know the reason this time and didn't much care. Rather than flinch or worry, she stayed kneeling in the dirt, weeding the overgrown rectangle of roots and vines that had once been a garden alive with color.

The summer sun warmed her bare arms as the breeze lifted her hair off her shoulders and kept it dancing in front of her eyes. Needing a drink of water and a barrette, she stabbed the end of the sharp shovel into the ground and stood. A break sounded good after an hour of getting nowhere on the massive yard-work project.

She made it two steps before shots rang out again, this time multiple and in bursts. At the sound of the rapid rat-a-tat-tat, she spun around, trying to judge the distance between her and the bullets. Her gaze zipped from one end of the open yard to the other. A thunder of noise she couldn't identify filled her ears and grew closer as she scanned the part of the two acres she could see without moving away from the protective shield of the house.

A tangle of trees blocked her view to what lay beyond her father's falling-down property, but she didn't hesitate. Living in Seattle for the past two years had taught her one thing: don't invite danger. That meant moving. Smart women knew when to run.

She took off for the back porch as she tapped the pockets of her cargo shorts in search of her phone. Empty. Maybe that was for the best, since what passed for police on the island didn't exactly fill her with a sense of security. More like dread.

Her foot hit the bottom step right as the hair on the back of her neck stirred. That only made her jog faster. Anxiety rocketed through her as she reached for the door. Just as she tugged she heard it—heavy breathing, and not hers. She whipped her head around in time to see someone barreling toward her. Broad shoulders and big. Male and fast.

Her hand slipped on the knob, but she turned it. She managed to open the door an inch before a man's hand slammed against the frame by her head. The heat from his body radiated against her back as panic swamped her. She opened her mouth to scream, but a hand clamped over her face, blocking the sound.

"I'm not going to hurt you." The harsh whisper brushed across her ear.

Yeah, no way was she believing that.

She kicked out and shoved. Flailed and tried to run again, this time for the tree line. She would not go out like this. She'd always joked that if she stayed on Calapan she'd die. She refused to let that prediction come true.

She elbowed him in the stomach and heard him swear in response. Another shot or two like that and she might be able to put some distance between them and get inside. Gathering all her strength, she drew her arm forward again and pushed back. She hit nothing but air.

One minute she stood locked in an epic battle on the porch. The next, her attacker reached around her and got the door open. He propelled her forward, slamming the door behind them and locking them both inside.

He held up his hands as he stared at her with big blue eyes. "Please listen to me."

He could beg all he wanted. The dimple, those shoulders, the objective cuteness…she wasn't buying any of it. She'd never been charmed by a handsome face before and wasn't starting now.

If he wanted a fight, fine. She'd give him one. Without thinking or analyzing, almost on autopilot, she ran for the small family room on the far side of the kitchen. Guns didn't scare her, because they were a way of life on Calapan. Growing up here, she'd learned how to shoot. Cans, mostly, but she didn't plan on telling her attacker about that limitation.

Footsteps beat in time with hers. She ran. He stalked. He kept talking—something about needing her help— but she blocked it all out, her only thought being to find that rifle. There was a Glock around here, too.

"Ma'am, slow down for a second."

Not likely. She put a couch between them as she tried to remember where she had left the guns after she moved them around this morning. Her mind flipped to the fireplace, and a quick glance revealed one leaning against the mantel. The same fireplace mantel next to the attacker and not her.

Her mind raced with directions. *Draw him out. Let him talk.* She skipped all of it. "Get out."

"I will not hurt you." He hadn't lowered his hands.

That didn't mean he couldn't. Her gaze dipped to the gun strapped to his hip and the trickle of blood running down from the edge of the sleeve of his navy T-shirt. "Then leave."

"My name is Cameron Roth."

As if she cared. "Fine. Leave, Cameron."

"I work for a group called the Corcoran Team."

She didn't even know what he was talking about. Her mind stayed focused on the gun, the blood, the shots and the fact that a stranger stood in front of her. The combination was all her brain could process at the moment.

"I don't know who this team is, but you can go find them." She bit back the tremble in her voice and tried to get the words out as quickly and clearly as possible. "I'll pretend this never happened, but you need to leave now."

"I can't."

Looked as though logic wouldn't work on this guy. She mentally measured the distance from her to the gun and wondered if she could get there before he put his hands down. "You mean won't."

"I need you to stop worrying."

That voice, all soothing and calm. It called to her, but she refused to trust it. Not when it promised a one-way ticket to getting injured…or worse. "That's not going to happen with you standing in the middle of my house."

"I'm one of the good guys."

"Says the man who grabbed me and dragged me inside." Her gaze traveled over him and she thought she made out another weapon tucked into his jeans and outlined by his slim tee. "Were you the one out there shooting?"

All emotion left his face. His blank expression didn't give anything away. "There was a problem."

Forget the weapon—with that nonanswer the guy should be a lawyer. "I'll give you the keys to the car. You can take it and—"

"No." At his bark, she took a step back and he moved in, closing the gap again. "I'm here on assignment."

"What are you talking about?" She had no clue.

This was the nightmare that wouldn't end. She should have stayed in Seattle and let the house stand abandoned. Her father was gone and she didn't owe anyone on Calapan anything.

"I rendezvous with my team in fifteen minutes."

Again with the team thing. "Be extra punctual and go now."

The corner of his mouth twitched. "I would, but I don't want to be shot."

She wasn't sure if he was laughing at her or with her but didn't like either option. "That makes two of us, Cameron."

Some of the tension left his shoulders as he nodded toward the couch. "Sit."

He had to be kidding. "No."

"I'm at a disadvantage here. What's your name?"

This guy just kept talking when she needed him gone. "You aren't going to be here long enough for that to matter."

"There are some nasty people after me." He lowered his arms, but his hand didn't venture near the gun. "I'm just hiding out here for a few minutes."

"Who?" If there were more people out there with weapons, she wanted to be ready.

His eyes narrowed. "What?"

"Who is after you?"

His gaze went to the rifle and lingered for a second before returning to her face. "Let's just say some of the people on this island can't be trusted."

Yeah, that was a lesson she knew all too well. "Understatement."

"What?"

She ignored the question because she had bigger problems. Now he knew where all the weapons were. That left knives, and grabbing for those gave her the shivers. "Just so we're clear, you're running around the island shooting and being tracked by someone and have no trouble manhandling me—"

"That didn't actually happen."

"—yet I'm supposed to trust you." Her voice got louder as she went on.

He had the nerve to smile at her. "Yes."

"I'm not an idiot." Sure, her brain kept malfunctioning and waves of fear crashed over her every two seconds, but she was not letting her world end like this.

"I never said you were."

"And I have a phone." She lunged for the landline. It had been disconnected months before, after her father died. But this Cameron guy didn't know that…at least, she hoped he didn't. "The police can come and you can explain your problem."

"That's not going to work."

She'd read somewhere that trying to form a bond with an attacker sometimes helped humanize the victim. Since she was the victim, she was willing to try anything. "Tell me why, Cameron."

"You can call me Cam."

Apparently the bond thing worked. She shook the phone. "Talk or I'm dialing 9-1-1."

"That would be a mistake."

There was something about the way he said it. "Why?"

"The police are the problem."

A crack shattered the glass behind her, spraying it over the room. She ducked. Probably screamed. Just as she crossed her arm over her head, a heavy weight crashed into her. She hit the floor and skidded across it with Cameron on top of her.

When they stopped, he pinned her down. The second their bodies touched she started moving. She shifted her legs and tried to knee him anywhere it would hurt. He caught her leg and held a hand up as if to tell her to be quiet. The whole time his gaze scanned the room and his gun dug into her stomach.

Through all the kicking and squirming, the silence finally registered in her brain. She picked up his breathing and heard her own hammering in her ears. Other than that, nothing. No more shooting. No yelling.

He leaned up on his elbow and glanced down with their faces only inches apart. "Are you okay?"

"No."

He lifted his body off her and looked down the slim space between them. "You're hit?"

"I mean mentally." When she realized Cam's body shielded hers, that he was protecting, not attacking, she let the backs of her hands fall against the dusty floor. "I don't understand what's happening."

"That makes two of us." He shifted his body to the side as he slipped the gun out of its holster.

"Who is shooting at you now?" And why had Cam brought the person to her doorstep?

He crawled over to the one remaining intact family room window, ignoring the broken glass from the previous chaos and the crunching under his knees. "Your police chief."

Chief Kreider wasn't her anything. The guy had the whole old-boy thing down, all entitled and drunk on power…except for those times he was actually drunk. She was not a fan.

Following Cam, because he seemed like a good guy to hide behind, she sat on the other side of the window and peeked out. Three random men stood out there, armed and dressed in some sort of law-enforcement uniforms. None of them looked familiar and they all wore lethal shoot-first expressions.

That fast, she lost her ability to breathe.

Cam pulled her back down. "Be careful."

She only caught a glimpse, but… "You said you were fighting the police chief, right?"

"The guy standing in the middle of your yard."

"None of them is the police chief."

Cam's mouth dropped open. "What?"

"I think your problem just got bigger."

"And I think, since you're trapped in here with me, I'm not the only one with a problem." He reached behind his back and took out a second gun. Before she could scream or bolt, he handed it to her. "Do you know how to use this?"

"Yes." She took it but wished she didn't have to.

"Good."

"Not really." Something collapsed inside her. "I hate this island."

This time he did smile at her, full and sexy and the exact opposite of threatening. He opened her hand and put the gun in it. "Looks as if we finally agree on something."

For some reason she didn't find the look or his cuteness comforting. "Julia White."

"What?"

"I figure if we're going to die together you should know my name." It actually hurt to say those words.

Not that they affected him. No, he winked at her. "You're not dying on my watch, Julia."

"You sound confident."

"You can consider it a guarantee."

Chapter Two

Cam slid his body up along the wall and stood up. With his back covered, he peeked outside again. The men outside hadn't moved, which struck him as pretty bad planning. If he were in charge of the attack party, they'd be surrounding the house and moving in by now.

Thank goodness for amateurs.

His gaze bounced back to Julia. He couldn't help being impressed with the way she held it together. He'd rushed her, touched her and forced his way inside her house. Acted in a way that he begged to be punched. He'd watched the fear come over her, and before he could calm her, she'd controlled it. Taken the energy pinging around inside her and focused.

It was sexy as hell. So was the long wavy brown hair and then there were those big chocolate-brown eyes. Not that he had the time to notice…but he did.

He reeled those thoughts in because he had no plans to die today. He'd just made a vow to Julia, so now he had to figure out a way out of this mess without too much bloodshed. He'd brought the firefight to her door by accident. Even if it meant taking a bullet, he'd get her out.

She peeked around the windowsill, then ducked her head again. "Why are they just standing out there?"

"Good question." Cam kept his focus on the men. If he flinched they could move out of his sight, and he could not let that happen. Three of them, one dressed as the police chief and two in flannel shirts, which made them stand out in summer.

"I have another question," she said.

This time he glanced over at her. Seeing the pale face and the way her hand shook as she brushed the hair out of her eyes sent a shot of guilt through him. Still, he wasn't used to a lot of conversation in the middle of a shoot-out. "Now might not be the best time."

She checked the weapon before looking up again. "Why did you think they were police?"

Looked as though she talked when she got nervous. He tried to contain the adrenaline coursing through him enough to keep up the harsh whispering. "The uniform, plus the other two were at the police station. The chief knew I was coming. The usual."

She frowned. "That's the usual for you?"

"Uh, yeah." It all made sense to him, but in hindsight he'd played it too safe in the minutes leading up to his meeting. He could have checked identities through facial recognition, but that wasn't standard operating procedure for a job like this. It was supposed to be an easy witness pickup, not a death match.

Her attention did not waver. It stayed locked on him. "Who are you and what do you do?"

They absolutely didn't have time for that discussion. "Later."

And really, there was no easy way to tell her he worked for an undercover operation hired out to corporations and governments to handle kidnapping and threat situations. It was the kind of line that sounded like nonsense during a pickup in a bar. In real life it meant he lived in a web of secrets, lies and death. Not exactly the kind of information that was going to put her at ease right now.

"I don't think so." Her tone suggested she might turn that gun on him at any moment. "How about now or I'll go out there with them?"

"You think you'll be safe with a guy pretending to be police?" She'd already proven she was smart and quick on her feet. He didn't doubt she'd reason this through and agree…at least, he hoped so.

"Probably not," she mumbled.

"Then maybe we can take care of the attackers before exchanging personal info?" Seemed logical to him. He was about to point that out when the banging started again.

His hand went to her head. He pushed her toward the floor with his body covering hers. Glass shattered and rained over them. Edges clipped the back of his hands, but his long-sleeved shirt protected the rest. Drywall kicked up and a lamp exploded to his left.

The rapid volley gave way to another sharp silence. His head shot up and he took another look. The men outside still hadn't moved. Other than holding weapons at the ready and the glass shower, nothing had changed. When he looked down, Julia was already moving.

She visibly swallowed as she sat up. "Okay, we'll talk later."

He liked her style. "Exactly."

"Now what?"

"That was a warning shot." If they wanted to do real damage, to shoot their way inside, they would have. For some reason they stalled out there, and Cam couldn't figure out why.

He'd deal with that later. Now he needed an exit strategy, and the options appeared pretty limited. Running out the back door might work if she hadn't been wearing a bright red shirt. That would stick out with her streaking through the woods. Which led to the other issue—she lived in the middle of nowhere.

This part of Calapan consisted of lush greenery, dirt roads and little else. Her cabin sat with the water on one side and towering trees on the other three. That made running for help problematic. So shooting their way out won as the best scenario. And that was not good news.

"What exactly did you do to them?" The hand with the gun fell on her lap as some of the color seeped back into her cheeks.

Anger and blame—good. He could handle those. "My job."

"Could you be more specific?" The demand for information was right there in her tone and the flat line of her mouth.

He ignored both. "No." When she started to talk again he put a finger to his mouth. "Do not move."

"Where would I go?"

He decided to wait until later to explain hand gestures and go over the definition of the word *quiet*. Making sure he was dealing with three men and not more trumped everything. He could take them down one by one, but only if another line didn't loom behind this one.

Crouched and keeping out of sight, he shifted with quick movements around the cottage. Checked the side yards and the one in back where he'd found her a few minutes ago. It took about a minute thanks to the size of her place.

By the time he made it back to the window with Julia, he knew they were in serious trouble. "They're getting smarter."

She shifted her weight and sat up with her knees tucked under her. "Meaning?"

"They're spreading out." They'd finally mobilized. There was no reason to do that unless an attack came next. Cam still didn't know what was happening on this island, but it wasn't good. "They'll likely come in firing."

With her palms on the hardwood floor, she leaned forward. "You brought these guys to my door. Take them away."

If only it were that simple. But he did have a plan, and it involved taking her out of the cross fire. "Is there an attic?"

She made a face. "What?"

"Julia, I need you to focus." She could be angry and frustrated later. Now he needed her with him, because when the quiet broke this time he sensed it wouldn't stop until bodies littered the floor. "An attic?"

She shook her head. "There's only a crawl space."

He'd make that work. "We need to get you in it."

"Where will you be?"

He liked that she didn't balk or question what he wanted her to do. "You go up and I'll cover the downstairs."

"One against three?" She sounded appalled at the idea.

"I've beaten worse odds."

"Cal—"

"Cam." His temper flared unexpectedly. For some reason her not remembering his name dug at him, but he pushed the feelings aside. "Do you really know how to shoot?"

He'd handed her a gun, which was a risk. Now he needed to make sure she wouldn't shoot him in the head by accident.

"Of course," she said.

"Anyone but me comes near you, you shoot." He heard a noise. Faint but there. The attackers were closing in. No question about it. "That attic space?"

"Right." She crawled on her hands and knees until she cleared the sight line from the window, and he followed.

Smart woman with skills. She became more intriguing by the second.

They got to the short hall leading to the bedroom and bathroom and she pointed up. No string, but there was a small handle. He rose to his feet, nice and slow, while waiting for a new round of shooting to start. When that didn't happen, he went the rest of the way. He lifted his hand and felt nothing but air. On the second try, he jumped and his fingers brushed the handle. Grabbing it, he brought the door down.

Before she could argue, he took her by the waist and lifted. Her feet left the floor and she let out a half yelp before clamping her mouth shut again.

With only the rustling of clothing as noise, her body and then her legs disappeared into the dark hole above. A second later her face popped into the space. "Be careful."

He shut the door before she could say anything else. Now to bury the obvious entry. After a short mental countdown, he jumped, using the wall as leverage, and grabbed the handle. The yank pressed the hard metal into his palm but didn't come off. He only managed to knock the handle loose.

The second lunge cut his palm but did the trick. With a crack the handle fell off. He stuffed it into his pocket and hoped the shadowed hallway would do the rest to provide cover.

Then he moved. The corner at the end of the hall qualified as the perfect place. He could squat down and wait for the inevitable. Problem was, Julia sat right above. A stray bullet could ricochet and hit her, and he couldn't let that happen. That meant moving into the open, being more vulnerable, but he'd take the chance.

The kitchen worked as an alternative. He pivoted around the edge of the small island and hunkered down by the stove. Now began the game to see who would flinch first.

These guys didn't disappoint. One kicked in the front door and another stormed in the back. With the size of the house, they could have run right into each other if they hadn't stopped their momentum. They whispered and traded theories on his location. Cam heard it all.

Not seeing them, he had to concentrate on the voices and the footsteps to plot their positions. He had two in the small family room and one unaccounted for. Close enough.

When one came within range of the kitchen, Cam still held his position. Not moving. The preference was to take them alive. Much easier to question a breathing man than a dead one. Then the one who acted like the sidekick almost stepped on Cam's hand.

He sprang to his feet with an arm wrapped around the guy's throat as he faced down the one dressed as the police chief. The one who had all the facts and who'd sat in the office, pretending to be the police chief, which raised a lot of questions.

"Put the gun down." Cam issued the order as he backed his hostage into the family room and away from the hallway where Julia hid above.

The fake chief wore a smile that could only be described as feral. "You have been a problem."

No kidding. That was exactly what Cam got paid to handle. "Not the first time I've heard that."

"Lower the weapon and we'll let the woman live." One gave the orders while the other tightened his hold on Cam's arm to keep from being choked.

They'd seen her or guessed. Either way, them knowing limited Cam's options even further. Pretty soon he'd be down to about one.

Still, there was no reason to make it easy for them. "What woman?"

"Don't play dumb, Mr. Roth." That sick smile widened. "Yes, I know your real name."

That wasn't good at all. That wasn't the name he'd given as cover for the witness pickup. If the guy knew who he really was, he likely knew that the Corcoran Team was on the island. The mission could be blown. The same mission that was supposed to be exploratory only and not combat.

Just what they needed—more danger.

Cam's heel hit the back of the sofa and he stopped. "Where's the real police chief?"

"You need to stop asking questions and listen." The guy used a man-to-man tone, as if they were having a chat about everyday things. "You have five seconds before me and my men tear this place apart and grab the woman. Then we'll see how fast you talk."

"I'm looking forward to seeing that." The third man stepped in from a room in the back.

Cam guessed he had found a window. Didn't really matter how he got there. Problem was, the odds had just switched to three against one. Not impossible but not his favorite. It meant he'd have to kill two and take his chances with the third.

He had to stop the chief first. "One more step and I snap your man's neck."

"You think I care?" He brought up his gun and fired.

The shot exploded in front of Cam. He felt a jerk and then the man he was holding fell at full weight against Cam's chest. He dropped him with a thud to the floor and came up firing. He nailed the one in the hallway in the shoulder and knocked him back. The chief dived to the side and Cam dropped down as he scrambled around the couch.

The scene moved in slow motion, but Cam knew it took only a few deafening seconds. As shots continued to ring out, he blocked the hammering of adrenaline through his body and the grunts and heavy breathing filling the room.

He turned to get off a covering shot and took a quick inventory: one dead guy on the floor and the chief missing. The wounded shooter stood in that back room and fired random shots into the family room that kept Cam ducking. He was about to take a diving shot when he saw the crawl-space door drop. Not the whole way but enough to be noticed if anyone was looking.

The creak of the hinges had the shooter looking up. It was the distraction Cam needed. The guy shifted just enough to aim his gun into the dark hole, and Cam fired. Nailed him in the head this time and sent him crashing into the wall and then sprawling to the floor.

Cam jumped to his feet and searched the family room

and kitchen. The place looked like a war zone. Shot-up walls and broken glass. A shredded curtain and papers scattered everywhere. He didn't even know where half the stuff came from.

But a clear inside didn't mean they were safe. He checked the porch and scanned the front of the property for any signs of the fake chief fleeing into the woods but didn't see anything, including the truck that had been out there a few minutes ago.

"Julia?" He didn't bother whispering or covering. The men knew she was there and now all but the fake chief lay dead on her floor. "Talk to me."

When she didn't say anything he stalked to the end of the hall and looked up. The gun appeared first, then her face. "That was pretty awful."

Her voice shook, but she wasn't throwing up, so he took that as a good sign. "Are you hurt?"

"I don't think so."

The shaking grew stronger and he worried about shock. "Any chance you could be more definitive?"

"My legs are never going to hold me to come down again. Maybe I'll just live up here." She glanced down at the guy lying below her, and her eyes widened. "Did you... Is he dead?"

"Very." And Cam didn't want her staring at the guy. Nothing good could come out of that. He tucked his gun into his waistband and picked a position that had her looking at him and away from the still body.

But she was already glancing over his head. "You killed two?"

"One. The guy in uniform took out his own guy and got away. So much for loyalty." Cam lifted his hands and caught her, easing her to the floor and not letting go until she found her equilibrium. "You need to grab a bag and change your clothes, or at least your shirt."

"Why?"

"You can't stay here." He pointed around the room. "This is a mess and I don't know why the guy was shooting, so I need you off Calapan."

"Normally I'd get indignant and tell you not to order me around, but I'm okay with it this time." She handed his gun back to him.

He slipped it into the back waistband of his pants. "I knew you were smart."

"We need to get to the ferry." She wiped her hands on her thighs and blew out a long breath. "We can take my truck."

Looked as though she had more bad news in front of her. He winced. "Was it blue?"

"Was?"

Cam didn't see a vehicle outside. Unless she had a secret hiding place, they could add another criminal charge to the fake chief's list. "The one who got away took it."

Her mouth dropped open. "Are you kidding?"

In light of the past few minutes, the response struck him as overblown. Probably had something to do with the reaction to violence. She didn't double over or hide in a corner, but she did latch on to odd things. He could handle that. "I'm thinking a stolen car is not the worst thing to happen to you today."

"It's a two-mile walk to the ferry and we only have four a day. We miss it and we're trapped here. On this island."

The bad news just kept coming. He pushed aside his plans to hunt the shooter down and focused on this problem. There was only one solution—call in the cavalry.

He glanced at his watch and pushed the button. The one that sent an emergency signal out to the rest of the men. "We'll rendezvous with my team and get you to safety."

"Alive?" She managed to load that one word with a heap of sarcasm.

He didn't let her tone derail him. "My promise to do everything to keep you safe still stands."

"I'm holding you to it." She stared at him as if needing further reassurance.

He didn't have anything other than his word, which was pretty damn solid, so he nodded. "Good."

Chapter Three

Julia led him through the woods. The trees soared above their heads, blocking the late-afternoon sun and casting a chill over her. Light filtered through the branches and spots of sunshine highlighted parts of the rough terrain, but for the most part they had to rely on her sense of direction as a guide.

As a kid she'd used the forest area as a playground. There she could hide from her father's alcohol-fueled rages and all the yelling. She'd breathe in the scent of the wet ground mixed with pine and be surrounded by calm, if only for a short time.

Being there now qualified as the exact opposite of calm. Her stomach tumbled and her nerves jingled, making her jump at every little sound. The chirping birds and the swishing as the wind blew the leaves around, usually soothing, just had her twitching.

Cam walked next to her, keeping their pace brisk. Every time she stumbled over roots or overturned rocks, his arm shot out and he steadied her. She appreciated the assist but really just wanted to get on a ferry and head for Seattle. Her father's estate and the selling of the house could wait. She'd figure out the truck and how to remove dead bodies later.

She shivered at the thought. When her brain hiccuped over the destruction and seeing all that blood, she turned to the very real issue that she had to let someone in authority know. That would lead to questions she couldn't answer and the possibility of getting in trouble.

But the police could question her in her small apartment back in her Belltown neighborhood, because she was officially done with Calapan Island. This time forever, because nothing and no one bound her there now.

The place was gorgeous but had never been anything more than a scary death trap for her. That used to be metaphorical in many ways; now it was literal. She'd had to walk over dead bodies with her backpack on her shoulders to get out of her father's old house.

But really, right now she needed something to take her mind off all the terror and violence. Mr. Tall, Dark and Oh-So-Good-Looking beside her needed to step up and help on that score.

"Say something." She issued the order and then went back to stepping over mounds of this and that on the ground.

He shot her a side glance before returning to his never-ending scan of the area around them. "Your shirt is bright purple."

Not exactly what she'd had in mind, but the comment was potentially annoying and right now she'd take that over noticing his firm jaw and general hotness. "You're critiquing my wardrobe?"

"I was hoping you'd pick something that blended in."

A solid response, but not a request she could make happen. "Every shirt I own is a bright color."

He looked at her again, but this time his gaze lingered. "Why?"

"Because I'm tired of blending in." She'd spent her entire youth trying not to draw her father's attention at the wrong time. Since he drank almost nonstop, that had turned out to be always.

But she was an adult now and refused to be defined by her father's issues. She just wished she'd been stronger on that point and had confronted him before he fell out of his boat, hit his head and died. His death left her with a mix of guilt and regret and more than a little bit of anger over all she had lived through and the baggage she still carried around.

Cam shrugged. "I thought you picked it because you looked so good in bold colors. They suit you."

Her sneaker slipped and she lost her footing. One wrong step and she turned her ankle as she bit back a string of profanity.

"You okay?" He faced her with both hands on her forearms.

She bit her lip. It was either that or grimace. "Yeah."

"Julia, I need to know the truth here." His expression went blank and his voice grew serious. "I can always carry you, if needed."

"That is not going to happen." She balanced her body against his, digging her fingernails into his arms as she shook out the sore ankle.

"You sure?"

"It's just a twinge." One that made her vision blink out for a second and her head spin.

When she moved her foot to the right, pain screamed through her. She'd done this a million times. Years ago she'd stopped running because of weak ankles. Well, that and because of her absolute hatred of running. But she knew the pain would ease if she stayed off it for a few hours and iced it down. She sensed neither was an option.

"By your own calculations we have about a mile and a half left to go." He looked up. "Daylight will fade and the ferry schedule will get in our way."

"Can we flag down a car?" A risky thought with gunmen racing around, she knew, but it was an option. Cam with all his superhero skills might be able to tell a legitimate driver from an undercover gunman. At least she hoped so.

He stared at her in that way a man did when he thought a woman had lost her mind. "In a tree?"

For a second she forgot he didn't know the area. Despite the could-charm-any-woman dimple and cute face, he fit in here. Had an outdoorsy look to him, and his clothes blended in. Certainly better than she did.

"There's a dirt road for emergency vehicle use only. The wildlife enforcement guys and police travel it." As soon as she said that last part, an alarm bell rang in her head.

"I'm not exactly looking for a run-in with more police or people pretending to be police." His fingers squeezed around her arms, then eased again. "But if the path is clearer you'll have an easier time, so we can try it."

Last thing she wanted to do was drag the danger out. Sooner or later the ankle had to go numb anyway. "I can keep going."

One of his eyebrows lifted. "Your choice is the emergency road or I throw you over my shoulder."

The shoulders, the face, the general hotness—she liked it all. The bossiness? Not so much. "You need to work on your negotiation skills."

"Why? I just won, didn't I?" He guided her to an over-turned log and helped her sit down.

Before she could say anything or think of a comeback, he dropped to one knee with his hands up her pants leg. Warm hands slid along her calf, then down to the top of her short socks. With a gentle touch he rotated her ankle one way, then the other.

The whole thing left her breathless. She didn't even scream when the sharp shock of pain radiated up her leg. For a guy who could turn and shoot without blinking, he could soothe by the simple touch of skin to skin.

She swore her vision blurred a little as she watched him, but somehow she found her voice again. "You could leave me here and go get the FBI."

"Tempting." He shot her a smile that could melt butter.

"We can't take the shoe off or it will swell." She was just babbling now.

"I know." He stood up and held out a hand toward her. "Come on."

She struggled to stand and almost called a halt to the whole project until he put her arm around his neck. The move let her fall into his side with him shouldering most of her weight and not putting any but the barest bit on the toes of her hurt foot.

"Better?" he asked.

This close she could smell him. A mix of wind and woods. Very compelling and weird, since smelling guys was not really her thing. She worked in an office and answered phones. She dated, but not much since breaking up with the accountant who had waffled between boring her and scaring her as he drank scotch after scotch after dinner each night.

She managed to nod. Not that Cam waited for her to

be healed or even ready. He had them moving again, this time at a slower pace, but not by much. They wound around piles of rock and across fallen branches.

With each step, the end of his gun dug deeper into her side. She didn't complain, because he was almost carrying her, all while watching the area and stopping every few minutes to check for something only he could hear.

When they reached the dirt road about ten minutes later, she slumped even harder against him in relief. "Here it is."

"This?"

She couldn't really fault the disbelief in his voice. She looked first down one side, then the other. The path was overgrown in parts. In others she could see the faint outline of tire tracks. But mostly they looked at mud and stones. Pretty big stones.

But she couldn't come up with another option. All the roads, some better than others, required a hike. Some of them serious hikes, complete with rappelling. She could barely walk. Jumping up and down mountains was out.

"It's the best I could do on short notice," she joked even though there was nothing amusing about their current situation.

He stared at her for a second as if trying to figure out her mood, then nodded. "This should be a bit more stable for you."

She didn't see how, but now wasn't really the time to argue. "Sure."

She moved away from him and put some weight on the sore ankle. It felt all twingey and only a few steps from shattering, but she tried to trick her mind into thinking it was no big deal. "I'm fine."

"That's convincing." He reached out and this time it looked as if he planned to carry her. "Come on."

The rumbling broke her concentration. The grinding of an engine and thumping and thudding as the wheels covered the trail. She'd never been so grateful to hear a vehicle. "A car is coming."

He stood stock-still. "No."

"What?"

"Truck." He wrapped his fingers around her elbow and pulled, half dragging her back into the cover of the overgrown trees.

Her feet slipped and the aching turned to a harsh pounding in her foot. But that was nothing compared to the knocking in her chest. Her lungs seemed to want outside her chest.

Pebbles skidded under her sneakers as she tried to gain traction. "How can you tell?"

"Different sound." He slipped an arm around her waist and lifted. "Come on."

Her body took flight and she wrapped her arms around his shoulders to keep from falling. She wanted to scream and argue, but that engine noise and the ambling of the truck drew closer.

They'd gone about ten feet in when Cam turned and dropped. His knees buckled and they went down. She landed on top of him in a bone-crushing thud. His landing had to be harder against the rough ground, but she didn't have time to think about it because the world started spinning.

He flipped her until she lay underneath him, covered head to toe by firm, muscular male. She looked up and followed his gaze. They lay sprawled behind two stacked logs. Peeking through the sliver of space between them, she could see the tires and a flash of blue.

It was her truck or one that looked very similar. Her fury at being robbed mixed with the very real horror of being found out here. She'd heard the threats the men made about her to Cam. They didn't need to use the exact words for her to know being caught by those guys was not an option. She'd go out shooting instead.

The truck door opened and black shoes came into view. The leg bottoms of the police uniform. Footsteps echoed on the dirt path as the guy walked from one side of the car to the other. When he bent down to touch something on the ground, her breath caught in her throat. Not a single cell moved within her body.

Cam also froze. His eyes darted as he watched the movements, but even his hands stayed still. He had a gun in one and she had no idea when he had brought that back out again after checking her ankle.

What felt like hours passed. Finally, the guy stood up again. She still refused to breathe. Her fingers tightened on Cam's shirt, balling wads of material within her tight fists.

She heard keys jingle. Probably *her* keys. And whistling.

The jerk.

When the guy got back into the truck and the engine revved, she finally let the air rush out of her lungs. Her head fell back against the cool ground and she inhaled the scent of peat moss. Getting her heart to stop racing seemed impossible.

It took another few seconds for the tension across Cam's shoulders to ease. Still, he didn't move. His head lowered and he looked down at her with his mouth hovering over hers. "You okay?"

She shook her head because that was all she could get out.

Chalk it up to the adrenaline or the moment or that face, but she gave in and did something totally unlike her. Her hands smoothed up his chest to his cheeks, and then she brought his mouth even closer. When he didn't bridge the gap between them, she did.

Her lips touched his and at first he didn't react. Didn't make a sound or do anything. Then his fingers slipped into her hair and held her still as he deepened the kiss. The touch hit her with a jolt of mind-blowing fever. He kissed her long and hard until that dizziness came roaring back.

When he lifted his head again, she could barely hold her neck up. Her hands dropped to the ground beside her head. "Wow."

He nodded. "Yeah."

But she had to be smart. "The kiss was a onetime thing."

"That's a shame." The corner of his mouth kicked up in a smile. "What was it for?"

"Not letting me die." Seemed simple enough to her.

Some man pretending to be a police officer was looking for them, and Cam hadn't hesitated. He'd tucked her body under his and kept her safe. He'd already killed a man rather than let him touch her. She didn't know how to thank him for those things or how to deal with the confusion rattling her, since he was the one who'd brought the danger to her doorstep in the first place.

"Now what?" She felt as if she kept asking that, but it still seemed relevant.

He brushed her hair away from her face. "We find my team."

"Are they like you?" She tried to imagine a whole group of hot undercover guys with guns, and her mind couldn't process it.

He frowned at her. "You don't get to pick another team member to stay with you."

"I didn't say—"

"You're stuck with me."

"You don't want to pass me off?" She really hoped he'd say no.

"You do talk a lot." His thumb rubbed over her temple.

Much more touching and she'd forget they were outside and in danger and return to the kissing that felt so good. "You don't like talking?"

"Strangely enough, I'm starting to."

Chapter Four

She looked like death by the time they got within a quarter mile of the ferry landing. Cam called in the team to have them rendezvous at a new position because he doubted Julia could make it much farther.

Not that she complained. No, she never made a sound except for a grunt here and there. But when they started down the grassy hill behind them, he heard her sharp intake of breath and called a halt. No way could she take the slope from here to the water, and she all but punched him when he mentioned again the idea of carrying her.

He liked her spunk and the well of energy she kept finding. Most men he knew would have dropped at the sight of two dead guys on their family room floor. She'd hung in there.

But she needed rest, which was why they sat at a picnic table behind a grocery market with her sore ankle resting on the bench next to him. The employees likely used the space for breaks, but right now he claimed it.

From this position he could use his binoculars to scan the marina. Sailboat masts bobbled and a cool wind blew off the water. People lined up on the dock. A group of men talked with each person as he or she stepped into line for the ferry.

Cam didn't know what that was about, but the lack of uniforms and the fact that no one had performed those checks when he landed a few hours ago suggested it wasn't legitimate. More likely this group was part of the one that had shot up Julia's house.

He scanned the faces he could make out and body types for anyone who looked like the fake police chief. That guy struck Cam as the leader. If they cut the group off at the top, the rest should wither or at least be confused enough that wiping them out would be easier.

He glanced at his watch. Before he could read the dial, she piped up. "The ferry will be leaving soon."

"You'll be on it." For some reason that promise sliced through him. He felt the cut through his midsection.

Which meant he needed to get her on that boat now. She was a distraction. A long-legged, sweet-faced distraction with a butt that held him captive and a drive that enthralled him.

He'd watched as other members of the Corcoran Team paired off. Marriage, engagements, living together, serious dating. Strong men who vowed to put work first bowled over by compelling women they could not resist.

The Corcoran traveling team had made a vow, too—keep moving and stay bachelors. He had no idea how the promises broke down with the other members, but looking at Julia, watching her trace a fingertip over a crack in the tabletop as her long hair fell over her shoulder, he felt an odd tug. One he planned to ignore, and that started with a no-more-kissing rule.

"Do you plan to roll me down the hill?" she asked as the finger tracing morphed into drumming.

He almost laughed at that. "Might be faster than carrying you."

She looked up long enough to glare at him. "No to both."

"You need to get away from the island." Cam was starting to think everyone should leave, because no one would be safe until his team figured out the random pieces of what was going on and put them together in a way that made sense.

"Will that matter?" Her shoulders fell. "If these men know who I am, they can track me down."

He hated that truth but liked that she kept thinking it through, thinking about the angles. That caution would keep her safe. "You'll stay in a hotel and use cash."

"For how long?"

He wanted to tell her a day or two, but that could be a lie, and he refused to get her hopes up. "However long it takes to make sure you're okay."

She glanced off to the side. Stared at the trash cans without talking for almost a minute. "It's not my house."

Whatever he'd expected her to say, that wasn't it. "What?"

"The house was my father's." She drummed those fingers against the table again.

The steady rhythm started a ticking in the nerve in the back of his neck. He reached over and put a hand over hers. "Okay, back up. Where is your dad?"

"Dead." She delivered the information in a flat voice.

He wasn't sure what to say or how to read her mood, so he went with the obvious response. "I'm sorry."

This was not his area of expertise. His birth mother had lost custody before he hit kindergarten. She'd held on just long enough to make him too old and unadoptable, according to state officials. He'd spent the rest of his youth passed around from one foster home to another until he aged out of the system and turned to the military for a more permanent home.

"I was cleaning the house out for sale, though I'm thinking that might not be happening now." She sighed as she opened her hand and let his fingers fall between hers. "My point is, anyone who looks up the deed will trace my father to me, and me to Seattle."

He was still trying to process the news and what it meant in terms of keeping her safe. "You don't live on Calapan."

"Not since I was smart enough to run away at eighteen and not look back."

"Very smart," a familiar male voice called out from around the corner of the market just before he came into view. "I hate this place."

Shane Baker. The Corcoran traveling team member who was the most likely to make a joke to get through a tough situation.

Julia snatched back her hand and spun around. Looked ready to jump to her feet, which was the last thing Cam wanted her to do with that ankle.

Shane and Holt Kingston, the head of the traveling team, stepped into view. Cam hated to admit they'd gotten the jump on him. Hated more the idea they might have seen the whole hand-holding thing.

"Whoa there." Cam put a reassuring hand on her arm. "They're with me."

She sat down hard on the bench again and glanced at him. "Huh, you really all do look like that."

He had no idea what she was talking about. "What?"

"Nothing."

Cam decided to keep the focus on the problem instead of whatever might be running through her head, though he did wonder. "Holt Kingston and Shane Baker, this is Julia White."

Holt shook her hand, then moved in beside her on the bench. "Your hostage."

That was the last thing Cam needed to hear. If they thought he'd messed up, they'd never let him forget it. "It wasn't like that."

She looked at Holt. "It sort of was."

Shane joined the group at the table. He sat across from Julia and looked her over with a frown on his face. "You okay?"

"She sprained her ankle." He'd also scared the crap out of her and killed a man in front of her, which had to have her mind blinking, but the team knew that from his check-in, so Cam didn't repeat it now.

This time she aimed her sigh at Cam. "*She* twisted her ankle and *she* can speak."

Shane barked out a laugh. "I like her."

"She's a talker." Cam figured they might as well get that out of the way because Holt operated on the say-as-few-words-as-possible theory.

Shane's smile faded. "Oh."

With that done, Cam turned back to the case. "What do we have?"

"No identification on the deceased. Connor and Joel are working on it from the photos and fingerprints we sent."

She put a palm on the table. "Who are they?"

Something about the way she held her hand out had them all quieting down. Cam had never seen anything like it. The team members tended to talk over each other when it came to handling assignments. Connor and to a lesser extent Holt and Davis, the leader of the Annapolis home team, could demand the floor with absolute certainty.

Before Cam could give a personnel rundown, Holt jumped in. "Connor runs the Corcoran Team. It's his baby. Joel is our tech guy. Both are back in the Annapolis main office."

She held up one finger. "Okay, one more question—"

Shane whistled. "I see what you mean about the talking."

"—who or what is the Corcoran Team?" She ended the comment by glaring at Shane.

There was a long-winded answer about undercover, off-the-books work. Cam went with the easier response. "We are."

"That doesn't really clear anything up." Her last word cut off before she looked at Holt. "And did you say you checked the deceased? I'm guessing that means you went back to the house, though I have no idea why you'd want to see that scene."

Holt nodded. "Yes."

"Have we figured out why these guys tracked Cam and kept shooting at him?" she asked as she leaned in.

"Not yet."

Cam could have listened to her rapid-fire questions and Holt barely answering all day. It summed up their respective personalities. But he knew from experience Holt's patience would expire, and that was reason alone to end this.

"We came here to talk to a witness who reported some concerns. Raised some questions about illegal drug running on Calapan," Cam explained, trying to keep the intel as neutral as possible.

"Who?" she asked.

Shane shook his head. "I don't think—"

"Rudy Bleesher." Cam ignored the stunned stares from his teammates. He was surprised he'd shared that information, too, but nothing made sense on this job. They'd come here for an interview and ended up in a shoot-out. Not the usual assignment. "She's from here. We aren't."

She snorted. "If it's about drugs, Rudy will know."

Holt's eyebrows lifted. "Because?"

"We went to school together, and the guy knew all about drug dealing."

Finally a piece of the puzzle that fit for Cam. If Rudy had started out using and maybe dealing and now wanted to turn in evidence to cut a deal or get out of trouble or whatever, that made sense. And they were talking about drugs in serious amounts.

Cam had been with the team for three years and had never gone after a run-of-the-mill drug user. But word was the operation on Calapan was serious business and served as a source for moving drugs up and down the coast and into Canada, which made it Corcoran business.

"You're sure this is the same guy?" Shane asked.

She started drumming those fingers again. "The island is thirty square miles, and most of that is wooded and uninhabited. Yeah, I know Rudy."

"We need to talk with Rudy and get Julia off the island." Holt glanced down at her hand but kept talking. "The ferry isn't an option until we clear these guys out, which means we need to find the real police chief."

"You know about him?" she asked.

"They were there when I got shot at." Cam thought

that part had been obvious but he guessed not. "They were watching when everything fell apart."

Julia flattened her hand against the table. "Which time?"

"The first, the time that led me to you, but you make a good point." Back then Cam had called the scramble code and they'd scattered. At that point he'd still thought they could grab Rudy and be gone without trouble. Talk about a miscalculation.

Holt looked through the binoculars and Shane re-checked maps on his watch. Cam waited. He could tell something ran through her head. Maybe it was the way she gnawed on her bottom lip.

The quiet stretched on for a few more beats before she exhaled. "I can take you to Rudy's house."

"No way." Shane clicked on the GPS function on his watch. "Give us the address."

"You'll never find it," she said in almost an I-told-you-so offensive strike.

Cam sided with Shane on this one. "We're pretty good at this."

He wanted Julia long gone and far away when they tracked down Rudy. The man wasn't where he was sup-posed to be this morning, and all hell had broken loose because of that.

"Fine." She shrugged. "Go to the fourth turn past the group of willows by the water where all the kids went skinny-dipping in high school."

Shane stared at her. "Maybe a street name?"

"There isn't one, to my knowledge. Rudy lives in a shack." She sent Cam that I-told-you-so grin she'd all but promised. "Getting mail is the least of his concerns."

"You win." Holt slapped a hand against the table and got up. He pointed at Cam. "You take Julia and look for Rudy. Shane and I will find the chief or at least clear the ferry area of suspects."

She shifted to look up at Holt, who now towered over her. "How?"

He smiled for the first time since he had sat down. "We can be persuasive."

"But first." Cam eyed Holt.

"What?" She glanced around, looking more confused by the second.

"Right. Sorry." Holt bent over and picked up a bag. He took out a bandage, then an ice pack. "Cam is going to set your ankle."

Her gaze flipped to Cam. "You know how to do that, too?"

The woman needed to have some faith. "My skills are endless."

RAY MINER STOOD in the ferry's ticket-buying area, just inside the building, so he could get a good look at anyone approaching the marina. But he was looking for one person in particular—Cameron Roth. The guy was supposed to be some superstar pilot who was good with a gun.

Ray had some skills of his own and was pretty sure he'd impressed the guy by shooting the man he was holding from right under his arm. But now he was down two men and Ray didn't like that at all. Cameron would pay for that.

Two more of his men returned from their search of the ferry decks after the most recent unloading. "There's nothing and no one left on board, but the waiting passengers are getting antsy."

"Tell them there's a delay and to come back for the next one." When his men stared at each other but neither moved, Ray saw the positives in eliminating a few of his guys without Cameron's help.

Ned, the bigger of the two and the one who usually did the talking, cleared his throat. "They're starting to have questions."

As if Ray cared. "We have the captain tied up and the rest of the crew believing I had to come in from Seattle and commandeer the boat because of the transfer of illegal goods in one of the cars. Have the crew inform the passengers that there is a search ongoing at the moment."

"What if someone calls the real police chief?" Ned asked.

"He's busy running around the island right now, and we have control of the phones." Besides, Ray liked this cover. He could get used to wearing the uniform. It went with the gun. "My bigger concerns are Cameron Roth and Julia White, the woman with him."

Now Ray knew her name. Knew the boss wanted her tracked down and brought to him. Apparently Ms. White didn't live on the island and wasn't supposed to be there. She was the type who liked to stick her nose where it didn't belong. She'd learn the hard way what a bad idea that was.

"They can't get far. We have the marina in lockdown and they're about to run out of ferry service. There's only one more after this." The one who wasn't Ned delivered the information.

Ray didn't remember his man's name, because it didn't matter. The guy's job was to not mess up as he followed orders. "What about a boat on another part of the island?"

Ned pointed to the boats docked around them. "Possible, but they didn't come in with a boat, so that should lead them back here if they want to find one. We also have a few guys watching the water and checking private boats."

"Do we have the okay to shoot?" the other one asked.

The guy suddenly became more interesting. Ray liked where his head was in this. "Not the woman. The boss wants her brought in and this Corcoran Team guy taken out."

Ned's eyes narrowed. "Why?"

"Just do it."

Ned shrugged. "I'm just saying it would be easier to kill them both. Set up some sort of lovers' argument gone wrong."

Ray agreed, but he didn't have the final say. Not in this. He took care of logistics and security for the business. He was the reason they'd been tipped off about Roth showing up in the first place. A guy like that, with his reputation and background, made enemies, and when a DC business associate heard Roth was headed for Calapan, he'd passed the word on. Ray had taken it from there.

But whether he liked this Roth guy or not didn't matter. Ray knew the guy was dangerous.

"Don't underestimate them. This guy Cameron took down two of our men." Really only one but Ray guessed it would be bad for morale if he told them how expendable they were.

Ned stared at Ray. "Roth couldn't get to you."

Ray would not let that happen. He would win that battle every time. "Not me."

Chapter Five

The trek to Rudy's house went easier than Julia had expected. Probably had something to do with the fact that Cam hot-wired a car and drove them most of the way there. He insisted on using the word *borrowed*, but she preferred being factual.

The rocky drive ended a good five hundred feet from the shack. Not that she could see it. The place was so much worse than she remembered. Tall weeds and overgrown trees obscured the building where it sat in a small valley.

In her memory she saw a small one-story building with a front porch. Now that she was older and bigger, it looked like a shed someone might keep in their backyard to store lawn equipment.

Cam pushed away the tall grasses and forged a path ahead of her. The way he trampled down a strip in front of her made it easier to walk. So did the combination of the ice, wrap and painkillers.

Then there was the view. Cameron Roth was not hard on the eyes. Walking behind him, she could see the broad shoulders and how they fell in a V to a trim waist.

He picked that moment to glance back at her. "This is a house?"

She had the same reaction to the falling-down place, but something about his tone struck her the wrong way. "Not refined enough for you?"

He stopped and turned to face her. "I was in the navy."

Okay... She had no idea what he was trying to tell her. "Is that code for something?"

"I've been in the jungle, on a ship for months at a time, crawled through mud and sat point in a swamp for days." He hitched his thumb over his shoulder toward the house. "A falling-down house doesn't scare me."

Then he started walking again. Snapped right back into undercover-protector mode.

She'd caught a glimpse into the man behind the gun. The ship and navy part made sense. The rest sort of blurred as it sped by her. But that was the most he'd shared. The only personal thing he'd shared, actually. She wanted him to keep going. "What did you do in the navy?"

"Flew missions."

And like that the window slammed shut again. "That's specific."

"It's as specific as I can be." They reached the area where the tall grass gave way to a shorter unkempt stretch of lawn right in front of the house. "Anyone else live here?"

Cam had led them wandering off to the side. A group of trees blocked their direct view, but she guessed the real point was it shielded the view of them.

"I have no idea," she said as she looked for any movement around the place.

Cam backed her up into the trunk of the tree and shielded her body with his as he talked. "When is the last time you saw Rudy?"

"Graduation, so, like, eight years ago." The years had ticked by and she'd visited the island as little as possible, but some things never changed and Rudy was one of those.

Cam's eyes narrowed. "How do you know he still lives here?"

Spoken like a guy who didn't grow up in a very small town. "A guy like Rudy doesn't venture very far. He sticks close to home, never gets a real job and lives with his mom."

Cam pointed toward the ground. "Here?"

"She died a couple of years ago." Thanks to the internet, Julia had a direct line to gossip on Calapan...whether she wanted it or not.

"You're sure?"

Cam didn't stop leaning and Julia had to fight to keep from resting her palms against his chest. "She was the high school gym teacher and her car went off the road in an ice storm, so the news made the rounds."

With a nod Cam took out his gun and took a step toward the house. "Stay back."

She grabbed his shirt before he could get very far. "He'll recognize me."

"He could be dangerous."

"Only if you try to take his drugs." Truth was, the outside of this place made her more nervous than the inside. Who knew what lurked about out here? But the house couldn't consist of more than two rooms. Cam could cover that without trouble.

"Anyone ever tell you that you have an answer for everything?" He sounded more amused than angry.

"I'm the one who lives here and knows the people." And she still didn't want to sit out here by herself.

"Lived. Past tense."

She had to concede that one. "You got me there."

With a hand on her wrist, he moved her clinch from his shirt to his back belt loop. "Hang close to me but let me move."

They didn't head straight for the porch. Cam guided them out in a half circle and they came up the side of the porch and stopped next to the door frame. He never put them straight in front of a door or window.

She guessed that was a safety precaution thing. She supported him using any and all of his training to protect her.

"It's quiet," Cam said in a whisper.

She'd expected music. She remembered Rudy blaring music. "Maybe he's gone."

"Huh." Cam looked through the curtain-covered window at the top of the door. "Maybe."

He turned the knob and the front door opened with a creak. It sounded like a bad horror movie. Other than a strange humming sound, she didn't hear anything. Most of the house was cast in shadows, but a stream of sunshine sneaked in and dust danced wherever it shined.

But the smell hit her. Rotten meat.

"What is that?" She guessed Rudy had forgotten to pay the electric bills and ended up with a refrigerator full of ruined food.

The stench made her gag. She put a hand over her nose and tried not to breathe, but that didn't work. Then she buried her face in the back of Cam's shirt. Still, the smell got in her senses. It was like a living, breathing thing and it slowly choked the life out of her.

Cam started backing up. "Go stand outside."

"Why? I don't…" Her gaze landed on the shoe and traveled up the leg to a knee. "Is that a foot?"

With his hands on her shoulders, Cam pushed her against the wall and out of the direct viewing line of the body. Not roughly. More like to rest her back against something hard. She wasn't sure if it was for protection or out of a concern that she might fall down. Because that was her worry, as well.

She shifted until she stood by the front door. They'd closed it behind them and now she wanted to fling it open and run outside. She looked at Cam and had no idea how he stayed so calm. He loomed over the body without any reaction.

Then he bent down. His hands moved quickly, going into pockets and picking through the papers lying around the body by using the end of a pen.

When he stood up, he shook his head. "He's been out more than a day."

She wasn't sure what that meant for his assignment. Her main concern was for him to get whatever information he needed so they could leave. "What happened?"

"Looks like someone hit him in the head with something hard." Cam's footsteps tapped against the hard floor as he came toward her.

"It could have been an accident." She hoped. Part of her wanted this all to be one big misunderstanding. Better yet, one terrible nightmare, and as soon as she woke up the horrible pictures in her mind would blink out for good.

"I don't see blood anywhere but on him, and whatever hit him is gone."

He sounded so sure. So much in charge as he spouted off his expertise. Normally that would bring her comfort,

but the more they talked about death and stood surrounded by it, the more her mind muddled.

She knew they should do something, but she couldn't
kick-start her mind enough to figure out what. "So, we
need—"

"We have to leave. Now." He caught her by the elbow
as he made his way for the door.

She didn't slow him down. Last place she wanted to
be was at this house with this awful discovery waiting
inside. In two steps she was at the front door. She opened
it, ushering in some needed fresh air.

Cam swore behind her. "I should go out there first
just to check."

As far as she was concerned, he was lucky she didn't
run out screaming. "Next time."

Her foot hit the front porch, and the lights registered,
flashing red and out of the line of sight from the inside
of the house. Chief Kreider stood there with a line of
four officers, possibly every officer on the island. All
had their guns up and ready to go.

She tried to make sense of what she was seeing and
couldn't.

"Hands up!"

The order crashed through her. The words registered,
as did all the weapons. The police were here, but instead of investigating what was happening with Rudy,
they'd turned on her. Maybe on Cam. She couldn't really be sure.

Cam stumbled to the door behind her, and his eyes
narrowed on their unwanted guests. "Wait. Who is that?"

She felt as confused as he sounded. The only thing
that overwhelmed the confusion was the lump of fear

clogging her throat. "That is the real police chief. Bud Kreider. Real name is Brian."

"Interesting choice to go with Bud." Cam stepped around her and out onto the porch. "We can explain."

If anything the wall of police officers closed in. Kreider moved to the front and his attention never left Cam. What had started out as an awful find morphed into something else. Julia's heart hammered hard enough to echo in her ears.

Kreider widened his stance as he took careful aim. "Put the gun down now."

"Damn." Cam made a face. Quickly, then it disappeared to be replaced with that blank, unreadable expression he seemed to have perfected.

Her gaze shot over to him. "What?"

"I have three more on me," he mumbled half under his breath.

She knew he'd come armed, but the answer seemed so odd. So unlike what normal people did and how they acted. "What?"

"Both of you, down on the ground now. I'm not asking again." Kreider and one of his men got closer. She and Cam had their hands in the air, but that didn't seem to matter to the police chief. He all but shook as he gave each order.

She rushed to explain, because between the anxiety welling inside her and the tension spinning around all of them, she sensed a rash action headed right for them. "We didn't do anything."

"Julia White?" Kreider lowered his gun as his eyes narrowed. "What are you doing here? You haven't been to Calapan in years."

Mundane chitchat. She could handle this. Maybe while

she did, some great plan would pop into Cam's head. "Cleaning up Dad's house."

"Out here?" Kreider shook his head. "You'll have to come up with a better excuse than that."

He might as well know. Refusing to look at Cam in case he disagreed with telling the truth, she answered, "We're looking for Rudy."

She held her breath and waited for the fallout.

"We? You know this man?" Kreider pointed toward Cam as he asked.

There was no good way to answer that question. She felt she did know him, sort of, despite only meeting hours ago. In the end she went with the answer that seemed closest to the truth. "Yes. We came to talk with Rudy, but when we got here and he was..."

"Julia," Cam said, his voice like a warning, and it was enough for her to stop talking.

Kreider was almost on top of her now. "What?"

He'd know in five seconds anyway. If he touched the door, the smell would hit him. Seeing the body, no matter how hardened he was from years on the job and all that drinking, should hit with a punch. She still wanted to retch.

"Rudy is dead." Saying the words didn't help. If anything they brought home the reality that he was gone.

Close or not, Rudy was a human being. Someone had decided to end his life. Julia was convinced of it.

Kreider snapped to attention. "On the ground." He motioned to his men with his head. "Check inside."

"Chief, this isn't what it looks like." It grated against her to show the guy any deference. He was younger than her dad, but she'd seen him in action. He liked to throw his weight around and threaten. Suggest he had more power than he did.

Cam took a step. The move didn't put him in front of her, but his body did shield hers. "You had a meeting with me earlier."

Kreider's eyes narrowed even further. "You're Gideon Rodgers?"

The name didn't make sense. How many did the guy have? "Cam?"

"You giving out aliases?" Kreider shook his head. "Julia, what would your daddy think?"

She had no idea. None of this made sense. She tried to replay every minute since she'd come inside after the attack. Cam had told her who he was. Cam had told her why he was on the island. Cam had brought a firefight to her door.

For a second she questioned him. Maybe Cam had set up this elaborate ruse all while protecting his drug operation on the island. She'd never demanded verification, which meant he could be anyone. And the extra name didn't help.

Footsteps sounded behind her and she glanced around to see a policeman on the porch. "Sir, we have a body."

Kreider took the gun out of Cam's hand and the other policeman started a pat down. "Is there anything you want to tell me, son?"

"I'm not Gideon Rodgers."

"Whatever your name is, you are under arrest for the murder of Rudy Bleesher."

She didn't understand Cam having multiple names and all the other pieces of his job, but she knew Cam had been with her all day and didn't have any idea how to get to Rudy's house without her help. The man she'd walked around with, the one who'd played rescuer every minute, could not also be a cold-blooded killer. She'd never believe that.

"He didn't do—"

Cam shook his head. "Julia, it's okay."

"That's not correct, but wait." Kreider pointed a finger in her direction. "You are one step away from being arrested."

Her breath caught in her throat. "I didn't do anything."

Alarms blew in the distance and a line of official-looking county vehicles headed toward the shack. She didn't understand how they got there so fast. Rudy's place sat away from the neighbors—who had called them? Unless things had radically changed, Rudy didn't have the type of friends who would check in on him.

"We'll go through everyone's statements down at the station." The officer cuffed Cam's hands behind his back and Kreider nodded his approval.

Cam shook his head. "I hate this island."

"That makes two of us." But hating Calapan wasn't new. Questioning her trust in Cam, even for a second, was, and she didn't like it.

Chapter Six

Cam knew he'd never hear the end of this. No way would Holt and Shane let getting arrested slide without giving him a load of crap. And he probably deserved it. He hadn't seen the setup coming.

That was what happened when a guy started thinking more about the woman by his side than the job in front of him. Lesson learned.

"You've been busy since you've been on the island." Chief Kreider flipped through the paperwork in the file in front of him. "You stole a car, we have all those weapons to deal with, and now we have three murders."

Julia's gaze switched from the chief to Cam and back again. "Three?"

She sat at the small desk outside of the cell. Cam watched her fidget in her chair. She'd crossed and uncrossed her legs ten times now and they'd only been in the satellite police office for about an hour. Long enough for Kreider to put together a file, apparently.

Good thing the Corcoran Team kept close tabs on that sort of thing. Anytime any name or alias got searched, it popped up on the screen back at the team's home office in Annapolis. That meant Connor and Joel and whoever else was there and not out on assignment were running checks and tracking his location.

Connor had put the elaborate system in place as a precaution. The work they did offered more danger than reward sometimes. Connor insisted they run drills, conduct fake searches to try to trip up the computer tracking system.

Basically, he wanted them ready at all times for anything. Cam appreciated his boss's paranoia now more than ever, because it meant Holt and Shane would have a position and some sense of what just went wrong.

"There are two bodies at your house, but I'm thinking you know that." Kreider spared her a frown before he went back to reading.

Not that Julia was content to be ignored. Her foot hit the floor and she turned in her seat, fully facing the chief now. "Those men attacked and Cam protected me."

"Cam as in Cameron Roth." Kreider nodded as he flipped another page. "Your friend here also has several names. Did he bother to mention that?"

Cam wrapped his fingers around the bars as he studied the small space. One cell and a place for a guard to sit, the place where Julia sat now. During the walk into this place, Cam had noticed an outer room and two doors leading to somewhere—he wasn't sure where—but this building on the outskirts of nowhere couldn't be a thousand square feet or house that many officers on a regular basis.

"I gave you the number to call," Cam said for the third time, suspecting Kreider would ignore him this time, too.

"Of your boss, who would explain. Yeah, I got it." Kreider shut the file. "I'd rather hear the story from you.

But first, you." He turned to Julia and didn't say another word.

She frowned. "Me?"

Cam's hands clenched tighter around the bars. "Leave her out of this."

"You're the one who dragged her into it." Kreider focused his attention on her. Didn't break eye contact. "Or do you and Cameron here have a relationship of some sorts that might keep you from being honest with me?"

Her eyes went dark. "What exactly are you asking?"

"I'm trying to figure out why Gideon…I mean, Cameron skipped our meeting and showed up at your house instead. Maybe this is a plan the two of you had." Kreider looked back and forth between them. "Though I can't figure out why you would want to hurt Rudy or what you two might be planning here on Calapan."

"You can't be this incompetent." Everything about this guy ticked Cam off. He had a look of practiced ignorance. From the oversize belly and stain on his shirt to the swagger in his walk. He looked like a man who had traded a favor for a comfy desk job long ago and hadn't worked in the field or on a real case since.

"I wouldn't call catching a multiple murderer incompetent." Kreider stood up. The look of satisfaction on his face mirrored the way he held his body, all confident and sure. "The Seattle police don't. There's a detective here to question you about some cases that look a lot like this one."

Julia stilled. Her feet stopped moving and her palms came to rest on the table in front of her. "What are you talking about?"

"He's making it up." But Cam knew he wasn't. At the mention of a detective, Cam's blood ran cold. He knew of one other man running around the island wearing a uniform and pretending to be in charge, and that guy was lethal enough, steady enough, to kill a man Cam was holding.

"You'll see when the detective gets here." Kreider did a little stretch, complete with a grunt. "He's been at the ferry waiting for you to get in. Apparently you slipped past him."

That clinched it. Detective, ferry…the guy who was after him was going to walk right into the station and grab him the easy way. Might just put a bullet through his head and end it. Cam feared what would happen to Julia then.

Now to convince Kreider. "You're being set up."

"Julia, now would be a good time for you to pick sides." Kreider nodded in Cam's direction. "Is this really the guy you want to tie your future to?"

"He saved me."

Kreider shook his head and shot her a look of pity. "Or did he make it look that way so he could really kill the two men with the Seattle detective? Maybe your so-called rescuer is really a man on the run and he's using you."

She slumped back in her chair. "You're saying the guy at my house really was police?"

Cam could not let her thinking wander in that direction. "He claimed to be you, Kreider."

"Did you hear him do that, Julia?" Kreider kept up that pitying stare. "You think about that and we'll talk more in a second."

Silence screamed through the room the minute Kreider stepped out. Cam had hated the guy before. He detested him now, but the reason had changed.

Looked as though he had underestimated the other

man, as well. A few well-placed words and doubt filled her eyes. Cam could see the change wash over her as she questioned every conversation. "Julia, you can't believe—"

The chair squeaked as she turned around to face him. "Who is Gideon…whatever the last name is?"

This part likely wouldn't make sense to anyone outside the business. Cam's brain scrambled as he tried to figure out a way to deliver the information without sounding like a bad television show. "Gideon Rodgers. My cover name."

"Why did you need cover if you were on Calapan on an official assignment?"

She asked the right questions and didn't just agree with whatever he said. The smarts were so hot, but right now they had the power to trip him up even though he was telling the truth. "We didn't know who was involved. Rudy's intel suggested powerful people on the island were in on the drug dealing. That meant assuming the police had been compromised."

She stood up and walked over to him. Stayed just out of touching range with her hands in her pockets. "You see how everything you've done and told me fits into Chief Kreider's scenario as easily as it does yours, right?"

"Yes." Cam leaned in, trying to get closer, to will her to believe in him. "But if I'm right, we're about to be in the middle of a bloodbath."

The wariness didn't leave her eyes. "What are you talking about?"

"If the guy who escaped at your house is who I say he is, then he is after us, or at least me, and I don't think he cares who he takes out in this station to get to me." That guy wisely saw Cam as a threat and wanted him out of the way.

The attacker had killed his own man to make a point. He'd go through Kreider and Julia and anyone else. Which was why Cam needed to get out, get away from her before she became collateral damage, and find his men. They had to piece together what they'd walked into the middle of, and fast, before it exploded on them.

Some of the tension left her face. "What do you want me to do?"

With that question, delivered in a soft tone, relief washed through him. He bent over slightly as he blew out a long breath. "Come close enough so I can grab you."

"What?"

"We'll make it look like I forced you to let me out. We'll play it for the cameras, but I won't actually hurt you." It was the only way to keep from dragging her deeper into this logistical and legal mess.

Right now she had deniability on the criminal charges. She could, and he would make sure she did, claim that he kidnapped her. Anything to take away the sting of her being an accomplice.

"You still have to get out of the building," she pointed out.

She wasn't wrong and he'd thought that through. Being on the run would stink, but it was better than going down in a hail of bullets in the corner of this cell. "This is a police outpost. There's barely anyone here. And this guy was dumb enough to leave us together even though he thinks he can turn you against me."

"Okay, but…" She rocked back on her heels as she chewed on her bottom lip. "Even if you make it to the outside, then what?"

"I'll figure it out." He could run fast and far and hide in the trees while he reconnected with Holt. "Julia, I know this looks bad and I'm asking for blind faith when you barely know me, but—"

"Be quiet." She put her head in her hands for a second. When she straightened up again, a new determination thrummed off her. She walked to the far side of the room and hit the button. The one that opened the cell.

He heard a click and the lock disengaged. The cell door moved under his hands.

But this was the wrong way to do this. "What are you doing?"

"Picking a side." She held out a hand to him. "Let's go."

He didn't argue. He should have, but it was too late. Anyone watching the security tape would see she'd staged the escape. That meant his sole task now was to protect her.

After a quick look out the door, they slipped out of the room. He wanted to go right and storm through the front door. He didn't really see another way.

She pulled him to the left. "There should be a door to the parking lot from here."

With quiet footsteps, they walked down the short hall and into what looked like a closet turned storage of sorts. One with three lockers and civilian clothes hanging on pegs on the wall.

They kept going until they hit the door at the far side. Cam disengaged the lock and waited for alarm bells to ring. Nothing happened.

With the door opened, they walked into the cool dark night. More time had passed than he thought, but he had a bigger question. "How do you know about that exit?"

They flattened against the outside wall. Cam stared

across the small parking lot. Only two cars and one official vehicle sat there.

"I grew up here. I've been in the police station before." Her voice stayed flat.

For some reason her comment made him smile. "Misspent youth?"

"More like picking my dad up after he got caught driving around drunk." She pointed toward the line of trees to their left. "This way."

"Hold up." He caught her just before she cleared the side of the building and walked into the open area. He peeked around the corner. "It's clear."

They ducked and ran. He didn't have a weapon to fire for cover and had no idea where the fake Seattle policeman was lingering about, so they took off. No talking. Just darted out.

They made it the whole way and dived into the trees on the side of the lot before he remembered her ankle. She paced around in a circle now with a slight limp, likely trying to walk off the ache.

Guilt smacked into him. "You okay?"

She nodded. "That wasn't too bad."

He had the exact opposite reaction. "Actually, it was too easy."

She froze. "Meaning?"

Incompetent police or not, there was no way they should have been able to escape custody that easily. An alarm hadn't even sounded yet. "We need to find a place to hide."

JULIA POUNDED HER fist on one of the towering double doors of the sprawling two-story log home with the A-frame front. She was tired and hungry and two seconds away from being full-on grumpy. Her ankle thumped and the realization that she'd broken Cam out of jail kept running through her head.

She'd likely have a criminal record now. She, the person who led her entire life by the rules and without fanfare. She looked over and glared at the guy who'd brought so much trouble into her life.

His eyes widened. "What?"

"As if you don't know."

She was about to say more, but the door opened. Sandy Bartlet stood there. Her father's friend and exact opposite. He had more gray around his temples and lines at the corners of his eyes, but he wore the same wide smile he always did as he ushered them inside and wrapped her in a giant bear hug.

He stepped back and looked her up and down. "You didn't tell me you were back in town."

"Only to clean up Dad's house for sale so I can settle the estate."

Sandy and her dad had grown up together, raised like brothers. She viewed him as the uncle she'd never had. The one stable force in her life when her mother left and her father's disposition turned more and more sour.

He was the one who had given her dad a job and cleaned him up when he fell down. He was everything her father wasn't—successful and dependable being the main two things. He'd owned the shipyard on the island and made a fortune when he sold it to the company that eventually ran it into the ground and put her father back on the unemployment line.

Sandy squeezed her one last time, then let his arms drop to the sides. "I would have helped you, but whatever you planned on doing with the house might be impossible now."

Something clunked inside her. She felt it around her stomach. "You heard."

"The news is all over the island." Sandy put his hands on his hips and switched his gaze back and forth between her and Cam. "What really happened?"

The move had her jumping to make an introduction. She was half-surprised Cam hadn't done it himself. "This is Cameron Roth."

The men shook hands as Sandy talked. "I assume you know something about the shooting."

The need to protect and explain rushed up on her. "I was there. Men came in, threatened me, and Cam protected me."

Still, Cam said nothing. He stood there, unmoving, with his hands linked behind his back. Maybe he thought Sandy would turn him in or was too stunned by the inside of the house. Sandy didn't exactly go for subtle. There were large-screen televisions everywhere and overstuffed sofas. The man lived in comfort.

"Well, then." Sandy clapped his hands together. "That's certainly a different story from the one Kreider is telling."

"You heard from him?" Cam asked, talking for the first time since they'd stepped inside.

"He called right before you came to the door. Told me this wild tale about a jailbreak." Sandy shot Cam one of those man-to-man looks. "But instead of hauling you in, it sounds as if I should be thanking you for keeping her safe."

Julia had no idea what was going through either man's head. Sandy looked impressed, though concerned. Cam's expression had gone blank, which was really not helpful or new.

She zipped right to the basics. "We need somewhere to stay until Cam can figure this out."

"Maybe it's best if Cam explains to the police and you stay here."

Cam nodded. "Maybe."

"No." She was not going down this road again. He'd tried to lose her at the police station by making things look even worse for him. She couldn't let that happen. Not after the insane time they'd been through.

Truth was, she felt safe with him. And the tiny voice in her head kept repeating that she really didn't want him to lose her.

That part she couldn't deal with or understand. The guy thrived on danger. He was everything she wasn't. Still, the one place she wanted to be was by his side.

She pushed the topic. "Someone is framing Cam for Rudy Bleesher's murder."

"What?" Sandy's head snapped back. "Rudy is dead?"

"We found the body. That's where the police spotted us." It all made sense in her head, but as the words spilled out she could hear the oddness of it all. No wonder Kreider had taken them both in. The only real question was why he hadn't thrown her in a cell, too.

Sandy looked over at Cam. "Seems death is following you."

Cam nodded for a second time. "It does appear that way."

The whole quiet act was working on her nerves. She needed Cam to stand up and defend himself. She planned to tell him that the second she got him alone.

First she had to make an ally out of Sandy, which

shouldn't be hard with their history. "Sandy, please help. We need a few hours without questions or being chased."

"I'm not sure what that last part means, but fine." He held up one finger. "For one night only, and then Cam and I are going to have a serious talk in the morning about how to fix this and keep your name out of it."

That was the last place her mind went at the moment. "I'm not worried about that."

Cam shot her an are-you-crazy look. "I am."

"And that answer just bought you twelve hours, even though I want to question you both right now." Sandy let out a long exhale. "Take the two rooms down here. You can go wash up and I'll make something to eat."

Relief swamped her, nearly knocking her down. "Thank you, and thanks for the reprieve."

She sensed it wouldn't last.

Chapter Seven

No way was he staying. Cam didn't like the look of the place. From the outside it looked spacious and homey, all lit up with security lights as the night fell. And with a very impressive security system. Cam recognized the name and wondered what exactly he was walking into and if he'd be able to get out again.

Now he stood in a bedroom and watched Julia slump down on the bed. The wise thing would be to wait for her to fall asleep and then sneak away. But after all they'd been through and the way she'd stuck up for him, that seemed like a pretty jerky way to handle the situation.

Then there was the timing problem. The ticking at the back of his neck said he needed to move. Sandy might claim to give them twelve hours, but his loyalty was with Julia, not him. In Sandy's place, Cam would get her to safety and turn someone like him—with the questionable story and police on his tail—in.

She smiled up at him. "I told you it would be okay."

Man, she actually believed it. That was why it was so hard to hit her with the truth. Well, part of the reason. The idea of leaving her made something inside him clench. He couldn't get wrapped up in her or her life. He should get her out of the trouble he'd created for her and move on...but the memory of that kiss kept smacking him.

He wanted her more with each passing second. The driving need threw him off. He didn't operate like this. He never got involved during a job. He met a woman, they went out, they had sex, it trickled to nothing and he moved on. Just the way he liked it.

But he knew forgetting her would not be that easy. Which was why he needed to get out now. Because of his attraction and the danger. Nothing pointed to a good reason for him to hang around.

He inhaled. "I'm not staying."

"Why?" She shot the word back at him before he even finished the sentence.

"He can keep you safe." Cam pointed out into the hall and the general direction of this Sandy guy's family room. "He'll turn me in."

"But he said he'd help."

Spoken like someone who never dealt in danger and lies. He liked that about her. The girl-next-door sensibility of living her life without fear. Family troubles or not, she was grounded and not looking for a fast fling. He got that.

"I don't trust easily, Julia. Don't ask me to trust this situation. Nothing feels right about any of this." He sat down on the bed next to her when he should have been walking out the door.

"He helped raise me."

Cam took her hand in his. Let his warmth seep into her cold fingers. "You, not me."

She twisted on the mattress to face him. "You have to trust someone."

"That's not an easy emotion for me." In his whole life that sentiment had never really worked for him.

The first time he'd found a home was with the Corcoran Team. Joel was his best friend. They saw each other less now that Joel was back together with the woman who made him happy, but Cam still tagged along. And he hung out with Shane and, to a lesser extent, Holt. They were a team and he entrusted his life and safety to them, but those connections did not extend to people outside Corcoran. Not for him.

"You think it is for me? I grew up with a rageful alcoholic. I didn't exactly have friends over for playdates." She shook her head as if trying to clear out all the old memories. "I don't want you to go."

The pleas tugged at him, made him think about doing stupid things that didn't fit with his life or the need to keep her protected. "You'll be safe with Sandy."

Her other hand went to his lap. Smoothed up and down his thigh. "You make me feel safe."

The touching, the sound of her voice, the pleading in those big eyes. Cam was ten seconds from breaking. "Don't do this."

She nuzzled her mouth against his neck. Blew warm breath over his skin. He fought it until he couldn't, and then he turned his head and kissed her. Right there in another man's house, in a place with security but no connection to Cam.

His mouth lingered over hers, caressing and coaxing, before he pressed deeper. The flash of heat hit him straight in the chest. The need churning inside him kicked up and his hands started to wander over her.

It took every ounce of his strength and self-control to pull back. When that didn't give him enough space, he stood up. Paced around and thought about airplanes. Anything to take his mind off her face and the touch of those lips.

"Then I'm going with you." Her voice sounded shaky.

He knew that wasn't from fear. He felt the trembling inside him and tried to tamp it down.

"Fine." But he didn't mean it.

He'd have to be that jerk. Walk away the second she wasn't looking. Leave her where it was safe and warm and hope that whatever connections Sandy had—and Cam assumed from the look of the place that he had some power—he'd use them to help her. If not, Cam would circle back and take responsibility so she could be free.

Her eyes narrowed as she stared at him. "Really?"

"Go wash up and then we'll find some food."

"Was that so hard?" She got up and kissed him on the cheek.

He tried to smile and make it look genuine. "Nope."

She went into the bathroom. He waited until he heard the water running, then constructed a floor plan of the house in his head. He tried to figure out the most logical ways in and out of the house by the layout of the rooms he'd seen and the look of the place from the outside.

The only question was the alarm system. Sandy hadn't reset it before he ushered them out of the foyer. Cam had to hope that was still the case.

Being careful as he placed his footsteps, Cam walked to the door and opened it. He could hear a television playing in another room and could smell food cooking in the kitchen. He ignored the growl of his stomach and slipped into the hall.

He stopped, trying to get his bearings. It was too risky to go out the front. And if the entry was that way, that meant a side or back door would be in another direction. He glanced to his right and saw what he suspected was a closet. A quick check confirmed the thought. His only solution then was a walk toward the noise.

Between the size of the house and the fact that it had sensor lights outside, this would not be an easy task. He tried to dream up an excuse in case he got caught. The need for fresh air. Probably as plausible as anything else.

The television grew louder as he reached the end of the hall. Sandy stood with his back to him as he used the remote to dial around the stations on the screen that seemed to take up a third of the wall in the massive family room.

At least that task had Sandy occupied. Cam didn't wait for another distraction. He slid along the counter and headed for the door on the side of the kitchen. The French doors by the dining room would take him too close to Sandy, but this one had possibilities. Cam just hoped it didn't lead to a pantry. Would be hard to explain why he was hanging out in there.

He waited to move until Sandy laughed at something on the screen. Cam placed each step carefully and didn't take his eyes off Sandy until he had the door open. Once inside, Cam smelled the faint scent of gasoline and spotted the two cars despite the dark. There was a wide-open bay and a door at the opposite side.

Getting over there took a few seconds. Checking for wires or any evidence of an alarm took another two. The alarm panel next to the door showed a green light. Cam hoped that meant go.

He turned the knob slowly at first, then yanked the door. Cold air and misty rain slapped his face. He glanced up and saw the searchlight aimed at the lawn beyond.

Now he had to play the game of beat the sensor lights. Dodge and weave, keep low and not make noise.

He'd just picked a path when a figure appeared in front of him. Round face, backpack and ponytail…and a glare that could melt steel.

"Forget something?" Julia asked through clenched teeth.

"No."

"If you had asked I would have told you there was a patio off the bathroom in my room." She exhaled and it sounded harsh and ragged. "The bathroom is the size of most people's family rooms."

That was a weird architectural choice and now he regretted not slipping in there to check it out. "Didn't expect that."

"Obviously." She tightened her hold on the strap of her pack. "This is where teamwork comes into play. We work together and you don't need to sneak around."

It sounded good. Too good. "You need to stay here."

"Not happening. See, I turned the alarm to pause. You have about five seconds to come with me before all these lights and bells come on again." She leaned in closer. "And this time Sandy will call the police on you."

Score one for Julia and her overwhelming hotness.

A smart man knew when he'd lost. "Let's go."

RAY SAT IN the front of the van with Ned. They parked a good distance away, on the other side of a small hill. They could move in without thinking, but they waited. Watched the woman and the man run into the woods as the rain started to fall around them.

He was getting tired of following these two. From the ferry. The police station. This house. It was getting old.

Ned wiped a hand against the fog on the inside of the window. "Why are we letting them go?"

This was not Ray's decision. If he had a say, these two would be splattered all over the street by now. Hell, he'd only pulled out of the woman's house that first time because the boss tracked his movements and sent a message saying to let the woman go unharmed. Up until then Ray had had it handled and could have taken Roth without any trouble.

But he wasn't in charge...yet. "The boss wants us to follow. Watch from a safe distance."

"Why?"

The questions skidded across Ray's nerves. It was bad enough he had to listen to directions from the boss. Hearing his inferior question every move just added to the frustration boiling in Ray's gut. "He thinks Roth is not alone."

"You mean the woman."

"He's convinced that kind of guy from that kind of team would come here with other men. If so, we need to find all of them. Round them all up." Made sense to Ray. There was no reason to clamp down on only one problem when more scurried about. "The boss wants them all off the island."

"Are we still supposed to save the woman?" Ned asked as he traced the rain down the window with his finger.

"If possible."

"So, we're letting them go on purpose."

Ray was not impressed with how long it took Ned to reason that out. Maybe he'd picked the wrong second in command. Problem was, his first choice was dead on the floor in the woman's house.

Not many people got the jump on Bob, but Roth had,

which even Ray had to admit made the guy appear more skilled than they'd all hoped when they found out he was coming to Calapan to talk with a witness. Roth had fired one shot, a kill shot. Around the corner and in the middle of darkened chaos.

That one shot was the only reason Ray had held off on putting a bullet in Roth now. Sure, he had the boss's orders, but he really wanted Roth to suffer. See the life run out of him.

Ned looked over his shoulder. "Ray?"

"The boss always has a plan." And so did Ray.

Chapter Eight

It must be nice to have close friends. They'd walked and then gotten in a car. It had just happened to be there with the keys under the mat. Julia figured Holt and Shane were behind this. She didn't complain or ask questions, because the thump in her ankle had kicked up again. Once they were settled—and she hoped that happened soon— she'd dig into her bag and find more of those meds Holt had given her.

Cam took one last turn, then drove the car into the bushes. Right in. He had the old sedan tucked in between rocks and trees and now surrounded by shrubs. It was an interesting hiding place. Effective except for the part where she had to get the door open...and she had no idea where he intended for them to hide.

She recognized this area even though it wasn't one where she spent a lot of time. They were a few miles from the old shipyard where her father used to work. She could smell fish and feel the pickup in moisture in the air as they got closer to the water.

The place, like everything on this part of the island, had fallen into disrepair. Sandy talked about buying the land back and revitalizing the area, but Calapan wasn't exactly open to a big tourist crowd, which made the task a pretty bad investment. From what she saw of Sandy's life, he didn't make a lot of bad investments.

Unless Cam planned for them to hide in a tree, she didn't understand why he'd brought her here. "You know it's going to rain again in, like, five minutes, right?"

"Welcome to the Pacific Northwest." He held out a hand to her. The other one carried a flashlight.

Even in the darkness, guided only by one beam of light, she could make out his strong fingers. She grabbed on and didn't let go. "Where are we going?"

"I thought you knew every inch of the island." He marched, forging a path for both of them.

"I never said that." Then there was the part where she'd specifically tried to stay away as much as possible over the years.

At first when she did come here, usually to visit her father in the clinic, she'd always expected to see new buildings and new restaurants. A turnover in stores and fresh faces. That rarely happened. People who grew up here tended to stay here, except for the few like her who escaped.

Not many people landed here without any ties to the place. Most of the land was owned by a few, and neighboring islands like Bainbridge offered more of a welcoming community feel than Calapan. Here, neighbors sat miles away from each other and didn't want to get involved. Poor Rudy had found that out the hard way.

She thought about him and her mind zipped back to all that had happened in such a short time. That took her gaze to their joined hands and then to the sturdy man beside her who cradled her hand in a gentle hold even as he marched them through the tall grass and overgrown branches.

They broke around a cluster of trees and she stopped. Stood frozen to the ground. In front of her sat something that looked like a construction trailer. Old, with a rusted roof and a broken front step. She had no memory of the building, but it could have come after her time, before the shipyard wheezed its final breath.

Cam glanced at her. "Impressed?"

Kind of stunned, actually. "For a guy who isn't familiar with the island, you sure knew how to find this place."

She waited for the doubts to hit her again. She'd been swamped by them at the police station and unable to wipe her expression clean before Cam saw it. The strange anxiety over trusting him hadn't lasted long or lingered. It was just that Kreider had talked and she had listened and the words had made sense.

Then she'd remembered she was dealing with Kreider, the same guy who'd brought her father in to dry out but never arrested him. Who sometimes even looked the other way while her father drove around the middle of town drunk. A good old boy who protected his favorites and hated outsiders. The guy who found reasons to lock up anyone who was even a little different.

The idea of Kreider being too incompetent or too full of hate to see Cam as a protector was not hard to imagine. Kreider and Cam were too different, and if it came time to choose between them or pick one to believe, well, there wasn't even a contest. She picked Cam.

He clicked a button on his watch, and the dial lit up. "I'd like to wow you with my brilliance, but the GPS did all the work."

A handy tool. She noted that for a future purchase even if it did seem a little anticlimactic for Cam. She half expected him to have an invisible plane. "Okay."

"Holt found the place abandoned and set it up as a safe house for us after he cleared the area."

She was starting to like Holt. "Does clearing the area involve shooting a gun?"

"More like checking for vagrants and animals." Cam squeezed her hand. "We have a no on both."

They'd been so busy dealing with the two-legged kind of trouble that she hadn't even spared a thought for critters. The size of the raccoons alone around here could scare a normal person to death.

"Holt also dropped off some supplies." They went to the door in single file as they walked on a board across what looked like a deep puddle of water.

"Maybe I should have stuck with Holt." The quiet hit her and she glanced up in time to see Cam's jaw tighten. "Kidding."

"Believe it or not, I don't find that funny." He dropped her hand as he reached for his gun but came up with air, since Kreider had stripped him of his weapons hours ago.

She tried not to take the loss of contact personally, but he sounded as though he was serious. His tone matched his frown and neither said happy or anything similar. The idea that a man like Cam, with his confidence and control, could need reassurance struck her as funny, but she didn't dare laugh.

She went for damage control instead. "I don't find him attractive. Just you."

"That's better." He winked at her. "Stay here."

"Yeah, I know the drill by now."

He stopped before taking the last step onto the broken staircase. "You know we've only been together one day."

"It feels like months." That wasn't an exaggeration. She felt as if she knew him. As if deep down they'd bonded on some level that allowed them to fast-forward through the getting-to-know-you stage. Maybe that was what happened when the initial meet consisted of a hostage and shooting situation.

"I'm going to hope that's a good thing." He moved, balancing for a second on the piece of a rotted stair before pulling his body up to the deck.

He took careful steps. With each move he'd put a portion of his weight down. Once he heard the crack or the creak, he'd go forward. Almost sprint across as if to barely touch the piece of wood.

It felt as if it took forever for him to get to the door, but the journey only lasted a few minutes. Without looking back he turned the knob, then slipped inside.

With him out of view, the sounds of the night amplified. Crickets chirped and the leaves and branches swished and swayed. She could hear something scurry nearby but decided not to think about that. She blocked the critter just as she blocked the terror racing through her at the idea of someone sneaking up behind her.

She thought about that possibility and whipped around to confront whatever might be out there. Only a breeze greeted her.

"Are you okay?"

Cam's voice cut through the night and the nerves jumping around inside her. She glanced up to see him standing there with his hands on his hips, looking every inch a man in charge.

"I'm good." That qualified as a lie, but if she told him about the shaking knees and chattering teeth, she might accidentally distract him.

He held a hand out to her. "Let's get you inside and off that ankle."

He remembered. Of course he did.

She lifted an arm just as he leaned down. He had his hands under her armpits and her feet off the ground in no time. She spun through the air with her body pressed next to his. When the world came back into focus, she balanced against his chest with her arms wrapped around his neck.

"You're carrying me." It seemed like an obvious comment, but she wanted to point it out just in case.

"Yeah." The breathiness in his voice mirrored hers. Like everything else about him, that was way too sexy.

"I can stand." Not that she really wanted to at the moment. The feeling of his strong arms around her had that shaking inside her turning into something else.

"That's a shame." He pressed a light kiss on her mouth, then loosened his grip.

Her body slid down his. The friction had her breath hitching in her chest and her common sense in free fall.

Some of that shine of the moment dulled when they stepped inside. To think she'd made fun of him for demanding pristine accommodations. But this was not good. There was a cot with blankets folded and stacked on the end. She gave credit to Holt for that and the bag of food and duffel bag on the floor.

The rest of the place consisted of dust and cobwebs. Cleaning was not her thing, but neither were spiders. She shivered and not in a good way.

"It's set up to look abandoned," he said with more than a little amusement in his voice.

"Uh…" That sounded like crazy talk. A bit more in line with the scenarios she spun in her head about guys working undercover, but still a little weird. "What?"

"Holt cleaned it up, then added some charm. The idea

is that if someone comes looking tomorrow or any day soon, they'll see what they expect to see." Cam glanced around. "A stripped-down, no-one-lives-here building."

Now she was impressed. "You guys think of everything."

He shrugged as he stopped in the middle of the room. "Usually."

Something about that tone. She could pick up the nuance, which amazed her, since she missed all the subtleties of conversation at the office. "Meaning?"

He didn't say anything for long minutes. Just stood there staring down at the tip of his shoe. "Nothing prepared me for you."

Something spun around in her belly and she thought it might be fear mixed with a twinge of hope and a dose of excitement. "That sounds like a compliment."

He turned to face her. "Not that many things throw me off stride."

"Let me try now." Before he could say no or reason through the arguments, she had her arms around his neck and her lips on his.

The kiss dragged her under right from the start. She heard roaring in her ears, and excitement bubbled in her chest. Touching him, holding him, being this close filled her with a lightness she couldn't remember ever feeling before.

The throat clearing came a second before Holt's dry voice. "Am I interrupting?"

Cam jumped and put his body in front of hers. Actually held out his arms so no part of her peeked through except her head, which she kept moving to get a better view.

"Maybe I don't like Holt that much after all." She was only half kidding.

"That's what I was just thinking." Cam didn't sound amused at all.

HOLT COUGHED. IT was the worst fake cough Cam had ever heard. Didn't help that Holt laughed while doing it.

Then he held up a hand. "Sorry."

Somehow Cam doubted that. "Are you?"

Holt walked into the building. His shoes tapped against the floor and Cam wondered where that sound was five minutes ago. No one got the jump on him. He'd been trained not to let people sneak up on him. He'd failed that test in the past few minutes.

Further proof that being near Julia put him in a tailspin.

"Wanted to make sure you found the place and give you a status." Holt nodded to Julia as he talked.

"On what?" she asked.

Holt's mouth opened and closed again. Clearly the guy wasn't sure how to relay the information without debriefing Julia in the process.

Cam almost laughed at that, since this was the woman who had heard evidence against him and still sided with him. She didn't exactly cough up details in order to protect her own butt. She could be trusted, and he never thought that about anyone.

He could even admit it. "You can talk in front of her."

"Whoa." Holt made a face. "Really?"

Cam knew the reaction was about Cam's own issues, but Julia took exception. "Do you want a reference?"

"I wasn't... Never mind." Holt checked his watch. "The guy is following Shane."

"What are we talking about?" Julia sat down hard on the edge of the table. The confusion on her face came through in her voice.

"There's been a car shadowing you and Cam," Holt explained. "Shane managed a pretty stealthy switch and now the car is following him instead of you, but the driver doesn't know that."

An impressive maneuver and one Cam was grateful for. He'd picked up the tail early but didn't let his concern show. An emergency code to Holt took care of the problem, which explained why they worked in groups. Swinging some of these switches alone would be tough.

"Is it the police?" She did not seem even a little upset about the idea of tricking the police.

"Nah, it's a guy named Ray Miner." Holt slipped a piece of paper out of his back pants pocket. "Connor and Joel have been working on this."

Cam took the sheet and stared at the coded message. "Of course they are."

"This Ray is a mercenary type. Retired military who's had trouble in and out with drugs. He showed up on Calapan almost a year ago and now his bank accounts are flush."

"That's stupid." She looked back and forth between them. "Doesn't it make it easier to prove his guilt, if he is guilty of something?"

Holt shook his head. "They're hidden accounts. He's not an amateur and Joel had to dig to find them."

And that was the part that worried Cam. Kreider had ego issues. Cam didn't know what Ray had other than a uniform that didn't belong to him and some skills. "Ray is our fake police chief."

"Yeah, he clearly doesn't like you." Holt's voice grew

more serious as he talked. "He's been passing your photo around town, suggesting you're dangerous."

Julia linked her fingers together. Within a few seconds her knuckles turned white. "You think he killed Rudy?"

"Probably but he's not the leader type. Someone else is running this." Before Cam could ask, Holt filled in the rest of the details. "Kreider has gone missing. He was smart enough to remove the tracker I put on his car."

That did it.

"You're leaving in the morning." Cam stared at Julia but refused to debate this point. She'd stayed too long and he didn't trust Sandy. Cam wanted her back in Seattle in a hotel. The idea of her rolling around in crisp sheets did appeal to him. "First ferry. We get you to Seattle. If that's not safe enough, we put you on a plane to Maryland."

"Why?"

"The home office is there. The Annapolis group can watch over you. No one will think to look for you there." The more he thought about it, the more he liked the plan.

"One flaw." She held up a finger. "I've never been there and know no one there."

"That's what the team is for." Connor would watch over her. The women would take her in. Sure, he'd have to fight off all kinds of matchmaking attempts, but no one would be shooting at her, and that was worth it to Cam.

"You don't think that would be a little odd?" She looked as if she was fighting a laugh. "You dump me on these people and then stay here?"

"This is what we do." They rescued people and kept them safe. That was exactly what this would be.

"I wouldn't know what to do with myself."

She was missing the point, so Cam tried again. "This is not about comfort. It's about safety."

She rolled her eyes at him. "I knew you were going to say that."

This was not the time for this argument, but Cam was fine to have it. He took a step toward her, but Holt blocked his path. "Can I talk with you for a second?"

That sounded like a request, but it wasn't. Cam wanted to say no, but Holt would just threaten to kick his ass, and nothing good could come out of that situation to calm Julia's nerves.

Holt didn't even wait for an answer. He opened the door and stepped out on a solid plank on the deck. Cam closed the door behind him and joined his friend and team leader. And waited. A lecture would hit any second now. Cam could feel it.

"I like her," Holt said.

That was not where Cam had expected the conversation to go. But he was wary because Holt could easily be luring him in. "Okay."

Holt had both hands on his hips. "Anything you want to tell me?"

There it was. The circle around to the private stuff. Cam pretended he didn't get it and went right to the work angle. "We need to look into people in addition to Kreider. He has the connections, but I can't believe others would follow him. He's not the kind of guy who can command men for long." Cam wrote a list in his head. "There's this guy named Sandy—"

"No." Holt actually made a weird sound that came out kind of like a growl. "About Julia."

Yeah, this was The Talk. Cam braced for the rest of it. "She's pretty tough."

"Uh-huh."

"Bright, smart, confident. Doesn't scare easily." He

could go on but thought he'd said enough. Too much and Holt would shift this conversation into a place Cam didn't want it to go.

Holt's eyebrow lifted. "Pretty."

He said it, but Cam was not about to disagree. "True."

"Look, I've watched this whole scenario play out before. You're not the first Corcoran Team member to lose his head over a woman."

Cam knew all about the Annapolis office and how they got paired off one by one. Found amazing women and surrendered their bachelorhoods. He and Shane and Holt had joked about never drinking the water back at the Annapolis office because there had to be something in it that made reasonable men fall stupid in love. They'd also promised they would not fall into the same trap.

The danger and the missions didn't really allow for a home life. Cam wasn't quite sure why the Annapolis office didn't see it. Not that the women weren't great. They were. Every woman matched up well with one of the members. But the point was anything could happen. Cam didn't see a reason to take the risk when there were plenty of women out there who were fine with a no-strings relationship.

They were confirmed bachelors and Cam wasn't ready to let that go. "That's not happening."

Holt smiled. "She's hot. Like, way hot."

That was the kind of smile, as if he was mentally conjuring up Julia's face, that made Cam homicidal. "Holt, get to the point. Now."

"You know what happens next, right? You fall, hard and fast." Holt leaned in and his voice dropped lower. "You get tied up and ripped apart."

Cam had watched Joel suffer and squirm. He'd loved

Hope and feared for her safety. The combination had him spinning in circles and miserable until he won her back.

Cam did not want a piece of that misery. "I'm not involved with Julia in that way."

"You looked pretty involved with your hand up her shirt."

Did that happen? Cam just remembered his palm hitting bare skin and his mind imploding. "You're spying on me now?"

"I was going to walk up to the place sooner, but you were in midkiss. And not to question your skills, but it's not as if you noticed me." Holt held up a hand. "Which brings me to my point."

Cam beat him to the punch because hearing the accusation just might lead to a punch being thrown. "I'm not going to blow the job. I have never messed up a mission or put anything before the team."

"When it comes down to a choice between her or the assignment, you need to think about what you're going to choose." Holt wasn't whispering now. His deep voice carried on the still night.

"She's the assignment." The words rang hollow in Cam's ears. He couldn't sell the argument, because not one part of him believed it.

"That's just it, Cam. She's not. You dragged her into this." Holt's shoulders fell as he blew out a breath. "You made her a target when you ran into her yard and brought her into this mess."

The anger simmering inside Cam spilled over. He knew he was responsible. Knew and hated it, and having it thrown in his face didn't make the situation better. "Don't you think I know that? If I could go back and replay that and keep her safe from the beginning, I would."

"I know."

"But being shot at messed up my thinking." And once he'd had her he couldn't bring himself to store her. He wanted her by his side. He said this was to watch over her, but there were moments when he knew that wasn't true.

"Then give some thought to how this is going to end."

Cam got lost in the vagueness of that one. "The job or with Julia?"

"See, the fact that you're asking that question proves my point." Holt took off down the stairs. If he was worried about his footing, he didn't show it. He stopped one step from the water. "And because I'm your friend and a good leader, I put a condom in the bag."

"What?"

Holt smiled. "You're welcome."

The idea of being free to touch Julia... Cam couldn't even let his mind go there. "You're sending mixed messages here."

"I know." Holt didn't bother turning around this time. He just waved a hand over his shoulder and kept walking. "I'm just waiting to see which one you're smart enough to follow."

The longer he stood there, the more Cam questioned the answer.

Chapter Nine

Julia opened the duffel bag hoping to find chips, maybe some candy. She shoved some T-shirts aside and something that looked like a bomb. She had no idea what that was about. Mixing food with ammunition should be illegal. With her luck she'd eat the wrong thing.

A bit more shifting and she hit more goodies. The packet on top of a new pair of sneakers was not food. Not even close.

She picked the condom up between two fingers and held it, not sure what to do next. Instead of being excited or even grateful, she felt anger filling her. But throwing a fit was not her style.

This was some sort of go-to bag Holt had delivered for an assignment, and it came with birth control. Shirts, bombs and condoms. It was like some bizarre college pack.

The choices made her wonder exactly how Cam operated on a job. A guy who kept his pants zipped and his mind on the operation wouldn't need condoms. Could be she'd fallen for a pretty face with a sexy line.

The door opened and Cam stepped back in with the push of cool wind behind him. He shook his head and drops of water fell from his hair. When he looked up at her, he froze.

She continued to hold the condom. "This is interesting."

With a small shake of his head, he unstuck himself from the floor and came over to her. Crouched down even with where she kneeled. "That's Holt's idea of being helpful."

Cam made it sound so innocent. "He's your birth-control pusher?"

"He knows I'm attracted to you." Cam took the condom and slipped it into his front pants pocket. "He also gave me a lecture about keeping my mind on the job, so it's not clear what he wants me to do. Not that he gets a say."

Do... She'd been asking herself the same questions ever since that first kiss. Kept it private as she turned her options over in her mind. Knowing Holt and Cam were out there talking about her just felt wrong. "I'm trying to figure out if I should be embarrassed."

"No one was engaging in locker room talk or anything like that. Believe it or not, the condom is a new addition to the go bag. I'm trying to remember if Holt ever tried to help me out like that." He smiled. "I promise."

The twisting in her stomach started to loosen. Maybe she'd jumped to conclusions. Not trusting was a knee-jerk reaction for her. The doubting had become so ingrained it qualified as her go-to response. But, really, any person would wonder with those supplies.

Her father used to make a promise and then break it. She'd learned early on not to take anyone's word or operate on blind faith. Yet she'd done exactly that since meeting Cam. She didn't understand her reaction or how her attraction guided her when it came to him.

"I assumed that…" She flipped her hand around as she tried to find the right thing to say. It would be too easy to offend and she really didn't want to do that.

"Julia, it's okay." He reached over and slid his fingers through hers. "I get it."

"I guess it seemed like…" She groaned when the words refused to come. "Forget it."

"You have been hit with a lot of evidence that suggests I'm a liar and a jerk. Every time, you've assessed the facts with a cool head instead of jumping to conclusions." He caressed one of her fingers, then another. "You've listened even when it would have been easier for you to write me off."

The touch of his hand felt so good that she almost lost her train of thought. Almost. "And I've sided with you every time."

He shot her a smile. "I like that about you."

That sexy look had her insides melting. She didn't know how all the people he rescued withstood that. He turned on that grin, and the blood rushed from her brain. His effect on her senses had her breath coming out in pants.

"You don't seem so bad," she joked. And by that she meant he went to her head faster than any man she'd ever met.

"As for the condom, Holt's gestures, while well meaning, sometimes misfire." Cam sucked in air through his teeth, making a hissing sound. "He can be socially awkward."

Julia heard the respect and friendship behind the sound. "Does he know you say things like that about him?"

"I tell him almost daily."

The thought of the guys sitting around ribbing each other made her smile. "I thought maybe sex was part of the job."

Cam's eyes widened. "What?"

"You know, that you guys have a bet about who can score first. That you get together and plan strategy." She shrugged. "You hear about stuff like that. Usually when something goes very wrong or some poor woman finds out the hard way, but I see it here and there."

His frown didn't ease, but the touch of his hand against hers stayed gentle. "What kind of men do you know?"

She was starting to wonder that herself. "The usual twentysomethings. Guys I worked with. Went to school with. Friends of friends and setups. Randoms on the internet."

"That list makes me happy I'm thirty-three and not in the middle of the dating scene." He stood and drew her up beside him. "Come here."

She didn't say anything. She was too busy holding her breath when his hands landed on the small of her back and pulled her close.

"I am not married, engaged or involved," he said.

"That's probably a good thing in light of the things I've been thinking about you."

"I'm not— Wait, really?"

It was a nonstop action film in her head. She saw him and her, and there was nothing neutral about it. "Yeah."

He nodded. "Okay, well, you may as well listen to the entire list, then."

She took a big inhale and let it out slowly. "I'm ready."

"I have never, and I mean never, ever, had sex on an assignment. I do not go looking for bed partners from vulnerable people or people in danger." He shifted his legs until they straddled hers. "In fact, my attraction to you is a pretty big problem."

She tried to swallow but she forgot how. "Because?"

His fingers sneaked under the edge of her shirt, and his thumbs rubbed against her back. "I can't seem to control what I feel for you, and I keep trying. I'm thinking about you when I shouldn't be. What I see us doing together requires a bed and might result in traction. Possibly."

And just like that, any doubt still rumbling around her brain deflated and died. He wasn't a criminal or scamming her. He wasn't looking for a good time or boasting with his friends.

She could see the truth in his eyes and hear it in his voice. Under all that rescuing and protecting, past that dimple and that face that made her sigh, was a good guy. Decent and willing to do the right thing no matter what.

He cared about his team and would throw his body in front of hers without debate. She'd never known anyone like him. Growing up with her dad, she'd never understood that people like Cam existed. Not in her world.

But now she knew they did.

"I think we should break your rule." Her fingers went to the back of his neck and brought his head closer to hers.

"I don't understand." He whispered the words against her lips.

"That's because you have so many rules. Hard to keep track of them, I guess."

He smiled then. "Narrow it down for me."

"Maybe it's time you had sex on the job." Being bold

wasn't really her style, but with him she wanted to be honest and trust. To dive in.

He pulled back, but not far. "Julia, are you sure?"

"I'm attracted to you. You can tell that, right?" She brushed her lips over his chin and smiled at the way the scruff there tickled her lips. "It's wild and out of control and I can't think when I'm around you. That's a bad thing when guns are going off and I need to run."

One hand slipped up her back. "That sounds familiar."

"So, maybe if we just burn this off—do it and then it's over—that'll help." That was the least sexy thing she'd ever said, but she got the point across. Mutual attraction. Spontaneous and big.

His eyebrow lifted. "It's not going to burn off."

She had to agree with him there. She'd thrown in the phrase, thinking it would help make it make sense for both of them. She did not have a thing for sex and violence together and didn't want him to think that. "I don't think so, either, but we can try."

"I keep thinking about the word *burn*."

"Tomorrow something could happen and..." She nuzzled her cheek against his. "Well, I want a good memory."

Both of his hands found her shoulders, and his mouth went to her ear. "I'm not going to let anything happen to you."

His touch and scent, being this close and feeling so much a part of him, blocked everything else out. She forgot about the danger and men with guns. Ignored the horror she'd witnessed and the fear that still held her in its grasp.

She pushed all that aside and focused on him. "Right now I want something to happen to me."

"This is not smart." But his mouth traveled over her.

He kissed her in that space behind her ear that made her shiver. "Agreed."

"Anyone could walk by."

Her fingers tunneled up under his pullover jacket, skimming over his firm muscles. "Now you're reaching for excuses."

"You're right." Then his hands touched her cheeks and the rest of the world melted away.

She tried to hold on to the thoughts bombarding her brain but couldn't. Her body came alive with the sensations rocketing through her and around her. His kisses enticed her as his hands learned her curves. When he lifted her off her feet, she didn't hesitate. Her legs wrapped around his hips and she held on tight.

The room spun around her and a hit of warmth had her body tingling. He laid her down on the cot and climbed on top of her, balancing his weight on his elbows but never letting their mouths break contact.

The bed rocked and creaked. His head shot up. "Think this will hold us?"

"I don't care." She was too busy shoving his shirt and the one under that up his body and off.

The material fell to the floor, forgotten. She took a minute to skim her fingertips over his collarbone. He was firm and fit. Everywhere she touched, the heat of his skin burned through her. The kiss dragged on and his hands wandered. She felt the tug at her waist and heard the zipper of her pants screech.

She didn't care about any of it. She wanted her clothes off and her body rubbing against his. As if she said the wish out loud, he broke off the kiss and sat up. The cot wobbled, but he balanced his weight as he stripped her shirt off and unclasped her bra. He had his hands on her

breasts and his mouth traveling down her neck before she could find her breath.

Then they went wild. Hands toured and legs shifted. She felt him kick off his shoes, and her hands went to his belt. The buckle clanked as she opened the buttons and slipped her hand inside. She held him, moving her hand over him.

"Julia, yes." He held her head as his mouth took hers.

The kiss blinded her. Waves of heat crashed over her as the air rushed out of her lungs. Every nerve ending popped to life as she tried to remember every touch. But his expert hands and those long fingers took over. He caressed her. Slid her pants down and off, then covered her body with his again.

She felt his erection press against her. The energy in the room had her buzzing as her heart hammered a frantic beat in her chest. She heard a rip and he pushed his body off her by an inch or two to reach down between them.

Wanting the moment to last, she debated helping him roll the condom on. Thought about prolonging the intensity and need swirling around them. But she wanted this. Wanted him.

She helped him shove down his pants and welcomed his hips as they fell between her thighs. Sensations bombarded her as she drew her hands over him and felt his body start to press against hers.

His fingers touched her, making her ready for his entrance. The tips slipped over her in circles. Round and round until her hips swayed in time with his hand's motion.

"Julia, be sure." His words came out in a rush between heavy breaths.

She didn't bother to answer with words. She lifted her

hips and used her hands on his waist to guide him. Then he was inside her, filling her. Her inner muscles pulsed and her body hugged his. When he pushed in, then pulled out, she gasped. The sweet dizziness hit her as the friction of their bodies had everything inside her tightening.

She felt primed and ready. Need spiraled inside her and the slide of his body over hers had her wrapping even closer around him. Heat mixed with desire, and every cell inside her sparked to life.

As his rhythm picked up speed, her head fell back. She couldn't get close enough or hold him tight enough. Her mouth opened on his neck. Her hips bucked and her muscles stiffened.

Then her body let go. The pulsing and shaking continued as light washed through her. The tremors went on and she tried to count the minutes but couldn't concentrate long enough to do it.

When she finally opened her eyes again, her chest rose and fell on rapid breaths. She was about to say his name when the tension over his shoulders tightened. She could feel his body shift and hear the soft grunts as his warm breath blew across her neck. It took another few seconds for his weight to fall heavier against her and even longer until his muscles appeared to loosen and drop.

"Wow." He made the word last for three syllables.

At least he could speak. She tried and a wheeze came out.

"You okay?" he asked, sounding as though he was sure the answer would be no.

"Understatement." She wanted to hold him but couldn't even move. Her muscles weighed a good hundred pounds each and her eyes started to close.

He lifted his head. "That sounds good."

"I'm mostly amazed we didn't break the cot. At one point it felt like it bent in half." She looked around and saw the clothing scattered all over the floor.

"We got lucky there." He lifted some of his weight off her as his body hovered over hers.

"I'd tell you to remind me to thank Holt for the condom, but that seems weird. It might freak him out. I don't want to do that, since I need to keep seeing him." It sounded weird even mentioning it, but she was grateful.

Cam laughed. "Yeah, even though we're on the same team, we don't share everything about our personal lives."

"That's good to know." She was just babbling now. She was willing to say anything to keep the closeness going.

"I need to check the outside and you need to rest."

But it looked as if that wasn't going to happen. The only good news was Cam seemed concerned about her feelings. She couldn't really ask for more than that.

"Is that your way of saying you have to get up?" she asked.

"Didn't want you to think I was getting up because of some anticommitment thing." He skimmed his fingertips along her collarbone, then kissed the trail he made.

Her vision blinked out. That was twice. She'd never had a man affect her the way he did. "You're not?"

"You mean running?"

She barely knew what they were talking about anymore. "Yeah."

"Not with you." He kissed her lips again, light and sweet. "I don't want to go anywhere else."

Now, that was worth remembering.

Chapter Ten

The alarm went off on Cam's watch at dawn, just as he stepped out onto the porch and into the chilly morning air. He wanted to head back to bed and wrap Julia in his arms, but work called. Literally.

The message on the watch was clear. People roamed nearby. Holt sent coordinates and photos. He was the only guy Cam knew who could give a briefing via watch.

He bolted for the door, ignoring the porch and its dangers. Opening the door, he caught Julia in the act of putting on her pants. She zipped, then froze.

"What happened?" The concern was right there in her voice.

"We need to move." He didn't have time to be more specific. He could fill in the details later. "Grab everything."

He went to work on the duffel bag, repacking the weapons Holt had provided and reaching for two more to carry on him. Now he had guns to go with his knives.

As he loaded up on ammunition, she stared. After a few seconds she broke eye contact and then went to work. They moved in silence. When he looked up again, she stood there in jeans and a blue shirt, the darkest outfit he'd ever seen her wear. He guessed it matched her mood. It sure fit his.

Her fingers clenched the strap of her backpack and he didn't see any sign of abandoned clothes or food. She'd gathered everything in record time.

"You're quick." He tried to make a joke, but it fell flat.

All the amusement and satisfaction that had played on her face even a half hour ago faded away now. Her lips stayed in a flat line and tension pulled around the corners of her eyes. She looked ten seconds away from blowing apart, but she didn't whine or complain.

"I had a feeling we weren't going to get to enjoy a lazy weekend morning today. Not after how the rest of our time together has gone. We think we're in the clear, men come, we run, people get shot."

"Julia—"

"A few die and then we start all over again," she said as she adjusted the weight over her shoulder.

"Someday soon this will be over. You'll wake up and things will be normal. We can probably even work in a shower. Go out for breakfast. Be somewhat normal." He didn't even know why he said it.

After this job he had to walk away and let her get back to her life. She had a job and friends. She didn't move around and live in motels or worse. She'd probably never had anyone threaten her or aim a gun right at her until he came along.

His life was nonstop action with short breaks of boredom. He liked keeping on the move. It suited who he was and how he was raised. Talking about mornings and lounging flew in the face of his reality. Even mentioning the options seemed unfair to her.

But he wasn't about to take it back. He knew it was

wrong—he was wrong—but now that he'd given the promise he would make it happen, even if the calm only lasted one night. There was just something about her and the idea of lounging around with her and getting through the day without a surprise or telling a lie that intrigued him.

She took two more steps and loomed right above him. "Now that we got that out of the way, are you ready to tell me what's going on? The whole packing-up-the-weapons thing was a little unnerving. Is that normal for you?"

"Yes." That wasn't really a lie. He checked the weapons every day as a security measure. Most days he also took them out and carried them to a job.

"Okay, then maybe nothing is happening and I imagined it." She sighed. "I've handled guns my whole life but usually on the range, not on my living room floor."

"No, you didn't imagine it. Holt says someone is headed this way." Cam stood up with the duffel bag in hand.

"Is the person we're worried about here Ray?"

"Not sure, but we're not waiting around to let him in for a chat." Cam worked at keeping his voice even. He could feel the tension coming off of her in waves. There was no need to add to whatever anxiety pinged around in her since the name *Ray* had worked its way into the conversation.

"There's nowhere else to hide."

"We'll be fine." But just in case he took out one of the guns and handed it to her. "As a last resort only."

She checked the gun and kept it tight in her hand. "Not to sound bloodthirsty, but if someone comes near me who is not you or your team, I'm shooting."

He loved that about her. "That's my girl."

He cut off conversation then. He needed her quiet and focused and hoped the finger over his lips telegraphed that. Since she followed without question, he wanted to believe he got the point across.

They'd made it two steps when he heard the crack. He backed up to protect her and felt only air behind him. Spinning around, he watched her body drop as the rotten wood beneath her splintered. Her leg slid down and she let out a shocked cry.

The urge to drop to his knees and lift her out almost overwhelmed him, but he had to be careful. Too much weight in one spot and they'd both be stuck hanging there.

"Are you okay?" he asked, though he wasn't convinced she was in a position to answer.

Her eyes were glazed with shock. "I think so, but I honestly can't feel much at the moment. I'm blaming that on surprise."

"Stay calm and very still." He said it as much to himself as to her.

Not that she was moving. She balanced there, half in a hole with one leg tucked beneath her and the other hanging out of sight. He spied her backpack and the strap where it had wrapped around her neck. He did slip to one knee then, careful not to put too much weight in one place.

He kept up the steady stream of conversation, hoping to keep her calm. "We need to get you out of there."

"No kidding." She tried to move her arm, but the strap had it pinned to her side.

"Here." With quick and efficient movements, he unwrapped the strap and lifted the bag from her shoulders. "Are you cut? Did it break the skin?"

She already had a swollen ankle. Early this morning

before she drifted off, he'd elevated it and packed it with ice before feeding her more painkillers. He'd thought it would help her walk, but now the injuries could be much worse.

She shook her head. "I don't feel any pain."

He wasn't convinced that was a good thing. "Do you feel anything?"

"Anxiety and mind-numbing fear." She put her hands on either side of her hips and pushed up. The move had her wrist crashing through another piece of wood. "Now I feel a little pain."

"Stop." He wanted to yell but kept his voice to a whisper. Holt and Shane might be close enough to create a diversion and lure whoever skulked around away, but most likely not. Cam refused to take the risk.

She just waited there, shaking her wrist. "That wasn't my best move."

"You think?" He pulled the board away that trapped her hand. The old wood crunched and crackled under his palms.

She yanked the arm out and rubbed her opposite hand up and down it. "Thanks."

They still had work to do. He glanced into the hole and saw the sharp edges of the broken planks digging into her leg. He knew she felt that. She covered the winces and didn't whine, but that had to hurt.

"Can you lift up at all?" He put his hands under her arms and tried to pull.

She shook her head. "Don't, stop. Okay, that will lead to slicing and cutting. I'm pretty sure."

He had to break more of the wood. Grab her before she slipped farther under the porch. "We can—"

The voice stopped him. Faint and male but there. A

steady chatter as if someone was answering questions. Cam only heard one person, but that was enough.

They had company, and he'd be willing to bet it was of the unwanted variety.

The color drained from her face as she grabbed for his hand. "Go. Leave and find help. Just give me weapons so I can scare them off."

"No way." He mostly mouthed the words, but he meant them as if he'd screamed them. He would not abandon her to whatever visitor was headed right for them. Her suggestion made him want to punch someone.

The voice got louder. The guy wasn't doing anything to cover his tracks. That could mean this amounted to nothing more than an innocent hike, but Cam doubted it, since the message on his watch kept flashing a warning for him to leave the area.

Anything they did now would make noise. Attract attention. There could be more out there. Too many gunmen and it wouldn't matter what his skill level was. He couldn't take on fifteen and promise survival.

That meant he needed an alternative plan. He looked at Julia again. "Do not move."

She glared at him over that comment.

He took the duffel bag and slid it behind her, half obscuring it from view and balancing it against the door. Her backpack went next. Then he took a large step back, making sure his foot hit a solid plank before going any farther.

The warped wood wobbled but stayed intact. Then Cam froze. He needed to figure out where the voice came from. It took two seconds to locate the noise. Back of the house and coming around to the front.

Taking cautious steps, Cam headed in the opposite

direction. The entire time he held eye contact with Julia, sending the silent signal that he would not go far.

He held up a finger as he moved, not more than a few inches at a time. His steps fell without making a sound. He slipped his gun out of its holster, then put it back in again. He needed this takedown to be quiet and simple.

He lifted one leg, then the other over the cracked railing at the side of the porch. It was a five-foot drop to the grass. No big deal, and the overgrown weeds should cover the sound of his landing.

When his feet hit the ground, he ducked down and waited. It didn't take long. A man walked around the opposite side of the building. He held a gun and a radio. That explained the one-sided conversation. He was reporting back. To where was the question.

He got to the bottom step of the porch and stopped. He shook his head as if he couldn't understand what he was seeing, and then a smile spread over his face. "Well, look who's here."

"Help me." Julia's voice shook.

Cam had to block the fear in her tone and the memory of her shocked face as her body fell in a whoosh. She needed him clear and focused. He would dig her out with his bare hands if he had to. He just had to get rid of this guy first. And that meant biding his time until the right moment, so Cam pulled back and continued to sneak a limited peek at the scene unfolding in front of him.

The guy's gaze toured over Julia, then traveled to the porch. When he glanced around the area, Cam pulled back and out of sight. He had to do some scanning of his own to make sure no one sneaked up behind him.

"Where is he?" the man asked in a rough tone. "You were with a man yesterday."

Cam tried to place this guy. He hadn't been at the ferry, but there was no question he moved around the island with Ray. They shared the same dark pants, dark shirt wardrobe.

"He took off for the ferry, leaving me here to wait." Julia sold it. She sounded convincing and scared at the same time.

Cam figured she probably was both.

The man unhooked the radio from his belt. Cam couldn't let him click that button. He tore around the side of the house and hit the guy just as he turned to follow the sound. The knock vibrated through Cam. This guy was not little, but the hit sent them both flying.

The grunt registered as their bodies crashed to the ground and the guy's gun tumbled away. Cam bounced on top of the guy's side, then scrambled. He had to grab the weapon first. Get to that radio.

But this one wasn't going quietly or easily. He shouted for help as he took to his knees and crawled in the dirt toward the weapon. Cam grabbed the guy's leg, then his shirt and pulled him closer. His face scraped against the rocky ground. Cam didn't care if the guy's skin peeled off.

Just as Cam moved to straddle his back, the guy threw an elbow and connected. Cam felt the shot to his toes but ignored the shuddering through his body. He lunged again. This time he put his full weight behind it as he reached for the gun by his ankle, since the other had gone missing in the fall.

Cam hit the guy in the center of his back and sent him sprawling in the dirt. He pressed a knee into his spine as he crawled over him. Without waiting another minute, Cam snaked his arm around the guy's throat.

The guy kicked out and pushed his weight back, which sent them rolling. But Cam didn't let up on the pressure. He wasn't aiming to make the guy pass out. He needed him gone as a threat. That meant holding and tightening the grip as the guy slapped and choked.

Then his body went limp. One minute Cam fought and held on. The next the other man's body slipped out of his hold, boneless and unmoving.

Still fueled from the fight and ready for battle, Cam sat back hard on his butt and held up his gun. He shifted around, ready to fire if anyone else came running, but the morning stayed quiet.

His gaze shot to Julia. "You okay?"

She shoved against the wood around her. "Get me out of here."

"Yes, ma'am." Cam checked the guy for a pulse and when he didn't find one went for his pockets. He came up empty there, but he got the radio, and that would help.

"Cam?"

He glanced up at her again. "Yeah?"

"Now."

He knew the look of a woman on the edge, and she hovered right there. Without another second of thought, he walked up to the porch. With the danger past, the noise didn't matter. Cam held one board after the other, breaking them as he made space to lift her out. When he ripped the third one out, her body bounced. He took that as a sign.

Reaching down, he dragged her out while his hands still shook. "You're okay."

She fell against his chest with her arms wrapped around his waist. "I thought he was going to gain the advantage and I'd have to watch him attack you."

Cam smiled into her hair. "Have a little faith."

She pulled back and looked up at him. "We need to leave."

"Yes." Ignoring the aches and pains that now held his body tight, he held up the radio. "But now we have this."

The corner of her mouth lifted. "Advantage us."

"Exactly."

RAY STOOD AT the outline of a wall near the main staging area of the old shipyard property. With supply low but demand high, Ray had come in to see what was happening. Instead of following the work production, he watched Ned shout into the radio with his voice rising with each sentence. Ray didn't know what was wrong, but something clearly was. Not a surprise, since after months of smooth drug production, things had started to break down.

First, one of the workers asked too many questions and had to quietly disappear. Then Rudy balked at running errands and started to call in reinforcement. He'd had to be put down, and they were almost too late.

Now Ray had to deal with Cameron Roth and his team. The same team that had him driving around in circles, chasing the wrong car. This Cameron turned out to be a bit smarter than Ray had originally thought. He'd thrown off the tail without trouble.

Tired of being ignored and having his time wasted, Ray walked over to Ned. With each step Ray tried to remember the name of the guy who seemed to be missing from his informal mental check-in.

"Where's your sidekick?" Ray decided that was good enough to get the point across.

Ned shook his head. "He's not checking in and I don't understand it, because he'd been giving me a play-by-play."

"You were just talking to him." Ray had heard the conversation as the other man fanned out, checking the area in and around the old shipyard.

Not that taking the lead on the search made up for losing sight of Cameron Roth and the woman. Ray didn't like losing and hated being made fun of even more. Now he had to sit through a meeting where the boss ranted and raved.

The only way to appease the guy was to catch someone. Grab the woman or one of the team members. Ray still wasn't sure how many lurked around, but he guessed at least two.

When Ned didn't offer any additional information, Ray raised his voice. "Start talking."

"Craig cut off." Ned shrugged. "He was talking and then just stopped."

The shrugging almost got Ned shot. If Ray could afford to lose more men he might have done it. At least he now had a name to go with the stupid face of the guy Ned had brought with him to the operation.

"I am familiar with the concept of being cut off." It was the incompetence Ray couldn't handle. With every passing hour, it became clearer that losing Bob would cost the operation something. "Where was Craig when you lost contact?"

"Scanning the area."

Ray ground his back teeth together. "Be more specific."

"Checking some of the small outbuildings on the edges of the shipyard property. Apparently the place is lined with them. Construction workers used to live there and now some hunters do during season."

Now, that sounded promising. The island had numerous seasonal and low-residency houses. Roth and the woman could be anywhere, but for some reason he sensed they'd stuck close. Though it was only a hunch, he played it.

"Show me on a map."

"It's not on a map. Locals talked about these construction trailers all along the border with—"

That was enough talking for Ray. Besides, it was time he ventured out. "Show me and stay off the radio just in case."

Chapter Eleven

Many more incidents like that and she'd have to cut off the leg. First the ankle and then the jolting fall through the porch. Julia knew she'd been lucky to sneak away with a few scrapes and little else after that one.

Cam stopped fiddling with the radio he'd lifted off the dead guy. The thing had been silent since almost right after they grabbed it.

"You still doing okay?" he asked without lifting his head.

He was being sweet and acting concerned, but if he asked one more time she was going to scream. And that would be a problem, since they were trying to be quiet and stick to whispers.

They'd walked away from the safety of the building, since it no longer seemed that safe with a dead guy on the front lawn. The walk took them out wide and farther into the trees. Except for a few wild animals and any stray hikers they might come across, they were alone.

She knew Cam planned to dump her off at the ferry once he made sure it was safe for her to get on board. She knew that was ridiculous.

"The abandoned shipyard." That was the right answer, but she had to convince him.

He stopped and stared at her. "Excuse me?"

At least she had his attention. "There's an abandoned shipyard not that far from here. Plenty of buildings and places to hide. We can go there and regroup."

He stood there for a few extra seconds and then started walking again. "You're going to the ferry."

Time to take a stand. And that was what she did. Stood there holding her backpack, trying not to think about the breakfast bar she'd put in there even though her stomach growled every two seconds. "I can't."

He glanced over to the space where she would have been had she kept moving and did a double take. He spun around to face her. "You can."

His single-minded focus on this point trumped any stubbornness she'd ever shown. She knew this came from a place of protecting her, but still. "Sandy made it clear the entire island knows about Rudy and us breaking out of jail. Even if the ferry crew thinks I was kidnapped, they'll still call the police."

Some of the tension over Cam's eyes eased. "I see you've thought this through."

"And that's the best-case scenario. If they think I'm an accomplice, I'll be arrested immediately." She couldn't even let her mind go to that place.

Forget about losing her job, which she would. Conservative offices did not like having their receptionist's photo splashed all over the news in association with a series of murders. This was way worse. It involved charges and lawyers and statements. She didn't even know what, if anything, she could say. For all she knew, the Corcoran Team's identity was top secret.

So many questions…

"The plan was to sneak you on board the ferry." When

she started to talk, Cam just talked louder. "Shane will go with you, act as your bodyguard and clear every space."

He wanted to pass her off to Shane? That bordered on insulting. "Too risky."

Cam swore under his breath. "You sound like Holt."

With that piece of information Julia felt secure in thinking she'd win this argument. She just had to get Cam there.

"What does *your boss* suggest?" She emphasized the job title, thinking that might move the conversation along.

"We lie low."

Now, that sounded familiar. "Ha!"

Cam shook his head. "Don't do that."

Fine, she'd be quiet about winning this argument, but they both knew she had. "The shipyard."

"The rain isn't letting up." He looked up into the trees. Rain fell, but the umbrella of branches covered them from most of the downpour. "We should be inside."

Not his most impressive stall, but she appreciated him trying to maneuver and analyze and think of ways to keep her safe. At heart, that was what this was. He had a singular focus in taking her out of harm's way. Usually she would agree to go. She was not the martyr type, but none of the solutions sounded all that great.

The only option that worked for her was one where she stayed with him. Attraction or not, she did trust him to keep her safe and she trusted almost no one.

"There are buildings at the shipyard," she said, pointing out what should be obvious.

"We're talking five outbuildings and a warehouse, not to mention the partial walls and rusted-out ship hulls." Cam listed off the hiding places on one hand. "No one has cleared any of it."

Just as she thought, he knew all about the location. Probably researched it before coming to the island. Despite his attempts to act disconnected, Cam struck her as the never-miss-a-briefing type. "Last time Holt picked a place, I fell through the floor."

The corner of Cam's mouth twitched. Looked as though he was trying to fight off a smile. "You make a good point."

"So?" She held out a hand and let the rain puddle there. "We're getting wet just standing here."

He let out a dramatic exhale. "How's your leg?"

She didn't see any reason to lie about that. If he planned to use her injury as an excuse, he would no matter what she said. "A throbbing mess."

"You're not convincing me we should walk."

"Are you going to steal another car?" The guy was an expert at hot-wiring on top of everything else.

"No, much more of that and the poor people on Calapan are going to start shooting each other if anyone goes near a car that's not theirs." He rubbed his face. "But fine."

Without another word he started walking. He'd switched directions and now they headed toward the shipyard. She half wondered if that had been the plan all along.

They'd gone a few steps with the relative quiet of the forest cocooning them. She'd spent so much of the past few hours on edge that it was hard to train her system to calm again. She tried a few deep breaths. That didn't help. She thought about slipping her hand into his...until he started talking.

"Tell me about Sandy." Cam's gaze roamed around them as he never lowered that protector shield.

Some part of her had seen this coming, but still she hadn't really braced for it. "Why?"

"Conversation."

She knew Cam had to research all the angles. He believed someone with power was in charge, and Sandy's house suggested he had some. Still, he'd helped raise her and that made her defenses click into place "Nope, not buying it. You're digging."

Cam shot her the side eye. "You have trust issues."

She had to accept that argument. She didn't trust easily, and there was a reason for that. "You should have had my father."

Cam shrugged. "I didn't have a father."

"What?" Her footsteps faltered and she kicked a piece of wood instead of stepping over it but managed to regain her balance.

"Raised in foster homes."

He casually dropped the piece of personal information. She guessed he didn't share that much very often, and part of her was humbled by the realization. "Cam, I'm sorry."

"Don't be."

"That explains your whole man-as-island thing." The way he held himself. The loyalty to his team and the absence of talk about anyone else. The drive to do the job right. Something about those features combined with his need to get things done on his own and without input pointed toward a loner upbringing.

"My what?"

"You strike me as a guy with few emotional commitments." She saw reflected in him the same way she led her life. Free from entanglements. Cutting off meant less pain.

"True."

"I can relate to that." But now that she'd met him she had to rethink her strategy. A part of her wanted to open up and share.

In such a short time he had her turned around and wanting things she'd never wanted before. All while they ran and ducked and tried not to get killed.

It was surreal and weird and kind of messed up. She couldn't explain it, and for the first time in her life she didn't try to. She just went with it.

"One more way we're compatible," he said. Before she could chime in, he glanced at his watch. "Interesting."

She was beginning to hate that word. Up on her tip-toes, she tried to look over his arm. "What is it?"

"Kreider."

She looked around, half expecting him to ride in with guns blazing. "Where?"

"Shane tagged his car with another tracker, and this one stayed on." Cam used his fingers to zoom out and make the map bigger.

"I have a feeling there's more to this story." Kreider riding to the grocery store or something equally innocent could not be the issue. She knew it would take more than that to grab Cam's attention and hold it.

"He's not far from here." Cam pointed to two dots, one green and one blue.

She assumed they were the blue dot and feared they were about to change course one more time. "Please tell me we're not going to go hunt him down."

Cam winced. "Okay."

"Yeah, that's what I thought." She slipped the bag off her shoulder and unzipped. Taking one granola bar, she handed the other to him. "Any chance we can get through the next hour without you having to kill someone?"

He eyed up the bar and then her. "I can't promise that."

THEY SLIPPED THROUGH the trees and around obvious trails and potential landmarks, getting from the construction trailer to the area near what looked like a storage shed. Forging a route close to the top of the hill risked their position but also gave them the advantage of elevation if it came down to a firefight.

He could also see most of the valley, including the police car parked right where the tracker said Kreider's vehicle would be. A car and a building. This had possibilities.

The whole time Cam kept sneaking peeks at Julia to check on that ankle. He doubted her reporting about being fine was accurate. She had a tight rein on her anxiety and was tamping down the pain.

Another thing to admire in the woman. As if he needed more in addition to her strength, that impressive face, those intense eyes and a mouth that drove him mad.

Julia lowered the binoculars and handed them back to him. "Are they in there?"

He took another turn scanning the area. "Don't know, since we missed seeing the car get here."

She let her arm fall against the ground. Not hard to do, as they were down on their stomachs, dropped low and out of sight. "Is that a statement about how I slow you down?"

"About the rain, actually." It no longer came down in sheets, but the downpour had slowed their progress. Now the air carried a mist.

He was soaked to the skin because he'd insisted she

wear his raincoat. The jacket dwarfed her, but she did look pretty cute with the wet hair and oversize hood. Even now she kept pushing it back off her head to get a better view.

Of what? was the question. There were no humans around. No sign of Kreider or his men. No guns. Nothing out here to see.

They'd basically followed a ring around the outskirts of the shipyard. The construction trailer in one spot. The storage shed in the next. There were garages and other outbuildings, all outlining the far edges of the property line. Not that anyone could see a line through the trees and overgrown grass.

"Kreider should be in there, but why? It's the middle of the day." Cam meant to keep the analysis to himself, but he voiced the words.

"I guess calling out for him is a bad idea." She patted her hands against the wet ground, ignoring water running over her palms.

"It's tempting."

She glanced up and the hood fell back. "Since the rain died down, we could sit here and watch the car and the shed. Basically, wait."

Not really his style. Cam hated stakeouts and did much better with action than hanging around. "I want the man outside and Ray next to him. That would let us wrap this up, or at least start asking the right questions. If those two are in some drug-running operation, we need to know."

"Your office can't use some fancy satellite or something with infrared to detect bodies inside?"

"That's not as easy as it sounds." Cam liked how she thought. Go big. He had an idea on that score. "But we can flush him out."

A familiar wariness washed over her. "How?"

"Explosion." He used his hands to highlight the word. "Boom."

Her gaze wandered over his face as her frown deepened. "Are you serious?"

"Most of the time, yes." Off the job, no. On the job, pretty much always, which was why being with her had him floundering. He joked, she gave him a hard time... they had lose-your-mind sex. Not his usual assignment.

"Let me get this straight." She wiped her hair out of her eyes. "You're going to blow up that building with people in it."

Probably a bit of an overstatement, but he liked the sound of it. Unfortunately, Holt would say no. "A small explosion next to the car. Set it on fire, that sort of thing."

"You don't have anything a bit more subtle? Maybe a rocket launcher." Her voice dripped with sarcasm.

"I don't really do subtle." But he would kill for a rocket launcher right about now.

"I'm starting to get that."

"The goal is to figure out how many men Kreider has and where they are. We blow something up and get their attention." The more Cam spelled it out, the more he liked it. "Holt and Shane can round up bodies from there. Then we can finally start asking questions, which is what we were sent here to do in the first place."

"Your team is around?" The jacket rustled as she looked behind her.

"Close by."

"And you're going to bring everyone running."

Now she was getting it. "That's the point."

"Including the people who want you dead."

"That's why I want to see their faces. I can't fight what

I can't see, and there is someone above Ray. I'm sure of it." Made sense to Cam, but from the he's-lost-his-mind stare she was sending him, he figured that might only run one way.

Rather than run through the details, he got up to his knees and reached for the bag. The rip of the zipper echoed around them as he drew it down and the soft rain began to fall again. He typed one word into his watch to communicate with Holt: diversion.

The response came back in a second: no fireworks.

Cam pretended he didn't see that. He wanted big but went small. He pulled out an explosive device. It resembled a stick of dynamite but wasn't. It consisted of an internal chamber housing the chemical substance and wires. He could use a trigger from a good distance away. There would be a crash and fire. Enough to bring anyone hiding out running, which was the point.

"If you trip with that thing, will you blow up?" She sounded more intrigued than concerned.

He wasn't sure how to take that. "I have to set it off, so no."

"I still want to go on record as doubting this plan."

He put the pieces together and lifted the device into his arms. "If we flush the right people out, we can end this right now and we can sleep in a warm bed tonight."

He left out the word *together*, but it was implied. From her smile he thought she got that.

She gestured toward the car. "Then what are you waiting for?"

"I thought so." Cam took off then. He slid down the hill on the side of his foot, winding through the trees and dropping to his stomach when there was nothing to block a direct line to seeing him. He could almost hear Holt swearing from a half mile away.

Cam crawled the last few feet. Pebbles crunched under his knees and something sharp dug into his thigh. The wet ground helped muffle the sound, but he couldn't go in using pure stealth. Not with an explosive device in his hands.

He had neared the front tire when the door banged open. Not knowing if he was made or just unlucky, he tucked the bomb against his chest and rolled under the car. Footsteps thumped around him. He heard the car door open and calculated how fast he'd have to move not to get crushed under the tires.

But the engine never turned over. One of the guy's legs stayed outside the car as if he was leaning in to grab something. Singing while he did it. Then he stepped back out and slammed the door.

Cam held his breath until he heard the building door shut again. He exhaled, trying to slow the sprint of his heartbeat. Let his head fall against the cool ground for a second. Then he thought about Julia on that hill and started moving again.

He shimmied back out and set up the device. Placed it close to the tire on the far side of the building. The explosion should blow the car and rock the house. Bring the singer and whoever else was in there running.

Two wires and he hooked it up and, ready to go, got to his feet. His palms stayed on the ground as he looked around for the best place to hide. He had just pushed up when he heard it. The pump of a rifle.

"Stand up nice and slow. Hands on your head." The man laughed as he talked.

"You are not supposed to be here, but unfortunately for you, you are," another one said.

Cam ignored the comment about his hands and turned around. One of the men looked familiar. Cam thought he remembered him from the ferry. The other, no. Neither was Ray and neither looked to be in charge.

He tucked the detonator in his hand, hiding it. He had to get out of the blast radius. If he didn't, he had to buy time for Holt and Shane to move in close enough to fire. But even with them on the scene, it might be too late. These two men were smart enough to put the car in front of them and the building behind. It was a good plan until the vehicle blew up, and that was about to happen.

Cam tried some guy talk while he put a map together in his mind. "Just out for a walk, boys."

"Nice try. We know who you are." The bigger one pointed to Cam with the end of his gun. "People are looking for you."

"Where's the woman?" the other one asked.

Confirmation. They were with Ray. Cam didn't know who else they were with, but he made that connection.

Cam shook his head. "Don't know what you're talking about."

"There." The guy pointed to the hill.

Cam almost hated to follow his gaze, but there she was, on the top of the hill. Standing. Was she waving her arms?

Anger rushed over him and he almost missed the opportunity Julia handed him. With the men's attention switched, Cam moved. He took a few lunging steps, then dived over a bush. His finger hit the button as he flew.

A crack sounded behind him and then a wall of heat smashed into his body. He fell to his stomach with his arms crossed over his head and listened as the world exploded into chaos behind him. Yelling and the crackle of fire. One explosion followed another, and chunks of car rained down around him.

He didn't know how much time had passed until the thunder of noise died down. When he lifted his head again, Julia hovered over him with fear shining in her eyes.

"Cameron?"

"I'm okay." He had no idea if that was true, but he rolled over and didn't spy blood, and all his limbs were there, so he took that as a good sign.

"We're going to talk about that stunt later," Holt said from somewhere above him. "Lucky for you Shane caught the one guy who was thrown before he could get up and run."

Cam assumed that meant there were just the two. "And the other?"

"Gone, as in dead." Holt looked down at Julia where she sat slumped over on her knees. "You go with Cam."

She shook her head but didn't say anything. The lack of response fueled Cam. This was not a woman who stayed quiet. He struggled first to his elbows as the adrenaline gave way to aches and pains. Then he sat up.

"You created a diversion." She'd risked her own safety, and the idea of that had him reeling. He was half furious and half drowning in his attraction to her.

She picked at something on the ground. "They were on a beer run."

"What?"

"The guy took beer out of the car, got as far as the porch, then turned again." She let out a ragged exhale. "I guess he sensed you were there."

"And you rescued me." The idea held him in awe. He was not in the habit of needing someone to ride in and save him.

She shrugged. "It was my turn."

He heard Holt moving around and looked his way. The place looked like a war zone. A flipped-over car and a fire raging up the side of the shed. One body on the ground and fire and debris everywhere.

Cam cleared his throat. "You get to pick where we go next."

She touched his sleeve. "Sandy's house."

That was not really what he had expected. "Really?"

"You smell."

RAY LOWERED HIS BINOCULARS.

The shed, the entire area was on fire. He had another man down and one caught. He'd almost gotten off a shot and taken the runner out, but then more men appeared. Good thing the guard didn't know anything. He was stationed out here, checking the boundaries. He hadn't even done a good job of that. Too busy drinking, apparently.

No, like every other man on the job, this one couldn't be traced back to the boss. Ray doubted the guy they caught could say much about him, either. But he could answer some questions, and that moved up the timeline to take the Corcoran Team out.

At least he had the information he needed. Corcoran didn't send one man to grab a witness. At least three wandered around out there, making his life difficult. Ray could dispose of three. While he was at it, he'd eliminate the woman, too.

The boss was not going to like this. Then again, the

boss wasn't going to be the boss for much longer, so Ray didn't care. It was all a time game now, and the countdown had started.

Chapter Twelve

Julia regretted her decision within an hour of getting to Sandy's house. She'd made him promise before they ever stepped on the property not to call the police. But that didn't mean Sandy greeted them with a smile. He grumbled and took verbal shots at Cam.

With Cam in the shower, she knew it was her turn. Still, she tried to avoid the moment by hiding in the kitchen. She leaned down with her elbows on the marble counter and paged through the news stories she'd called up on Sandy's laptop. She had one empty bottle of water next to her and was most of the way through a second. Once she had a hot meal she'd feel better.

But she had to live through the interrogation first.

"You can do better." Sandy set his coffee mug down with a hard clunk as he slid onto the bar stool across from her.

Julia didn't pretend to be confused or dance around the topic. "He's not a killer."

Cam was a lot of things. Lethal, determined, caring, stubborn and a heck of a kisser. He could be difficult and demanding, but she knew to her soul he was not a killer. Not in the sense Sandy meant.

But Sandy wouldn't let the subject go. "You're telling me he hasn't killed anyone since you've been together?"

"Not exactly." She couldn't really avoid the details. The news was all over the island. There was talk of instituting some form of martial law and keeping people in their houses until the police could search. Ferry service had stopped for all but essential services, and word was that more law-enforcement officials would be pouring in soon.

None of that was good news for Cam or his team. As outsiders they'd be tagged as perpetrators. And Cam hadn't exactly been subtle in fighting his way through the island. Add in a potential drug runner working somewhere on the island and disaster loomed.

"That's it. I've waited long enough." Sandy slipped his cell out of his back pocket.

"No!" She lunged over the stove top and reached for the phone.

"This is the best option. You need to trust me on this." He pulled it back just in time and glared at her. "What is wrong with you?"

She wondered the same thing. That phone came out and a furious fire roared to life in her brain. Instinctively she knew she had to protect Cam at all costs. "You promised."

"That was a mistake."

This couldn't happen. She'd grab Cam and run if needed, but she didn't want it to come down to that. Sandy would see that as her picking Cam over him. He was that type of man. A very black-and-white thinker, he put a high price on loyalty.

"I trust you, and if you…" She didn't want to threaten,

and she'd walked right to the edge. "You need to trust me back."

"I have a problem with him, not you," Sandy yelled as he pointed toward the hall.

The water had shut off and she waited for Cam to come running. When he didn't she filled in the piece that still didn't make any sense to her. "He's with me."

Sandy's mouth opened, then snapped shut again. He stuttered and shook his head—things that were very un-Sandy-like. "Oh, Julia."

Pity. Great. She hated that tone and the sad-eyed expression. He'd been shooting it her way for years. "Please don't look at me like that."

"At the very least agree that when he heads out, you'll stay behind with me. Behind locked gates and doors." He wrapped his fingers around the edge of the counter and leaned in. "That man is dangerous."

As far as she was concerned, he had it backward. "Right now this island is dangerous."

"Because of him." Sandy's knuckles turned white.

"He has put his body in front of mine and risked his own neck to save mine. He's played decoy and lured attackers away from me." She could keep listing but ticked off the highlights on her fingers instead. "Does that sound like a guy who will hurt me?"

Sandy leaned back on the bar stool. "Why is he on Calapan?"

She wanted to ignore the question or at least dodge it. But Sandy deserved more than a shove off. "He came here to interview a witness. Apparently there's some intel—"

"Intel?"

"—that someone is running drugs, serious drugs, off Calapan."

Finishing the sentence was easier than admitting she sounded like a television show. After a few days Cam had her sounding like him, and that wasn't necessarily a good thing, since she barely understood what he was talking about sometimes.

"How did an interview turn into a shoot-out?" Sandy asked.

She grabbed her water bottle because she needed something to occupy her hands. "Rudy was the witness and someone killed him."

"You keep ignoring how your man is at the center of all this."

She let the phrase *your man* slide by. She didn't hate it. Being linked to Cam didn't scare her or upset her.

"Someone in power is at the top of this. There's a man on the island pretending to be a police officer." She peeled down the corner of the label and heard a rip.

Sandy never broke eye contact with her. "You know that to be true?"

"Yes." Only because Cam and his team had told her, but she would not get knocked off track. The need to test Cam's trust kicked hard inside her, but she pushed it back. He didn't have anything to prove and she had to keep remembering that. "Is it possible Chief Kreider is involved?"

Sandy sighed at her. "I know you don't like him."

"He has connections and knows the island." She tore the label in half.

"You're taking on your boyfriend's paranoia."

"She's smarter than I am." Cam stepped up right behind her with his hands on her shoulders.

She noticed how he didn't correct Sandy about who he was to her. Like that, all the anxiety curling into a ball in her stomach disappeared in a flash. His voice had the power to do that to her.

She pressed a hand over his. "Cam."

He came around her side to stand directly in front of Sandy. "Is there something you want to ask me?"

"I'm worried about Julia," Sandy said before Cam finished the question.

Cam nodded. "So am I."

"I can get her off the island."

She listened to the verbal volleys until a migraine started to form over her eyes. "I'm sitting right here."

Silence flashed through the room. The refrigerator hummed and a clock ticked somewhere, but no one moved.

Finally Sandy stood up and put the cell back in his pocket. "You both look ready to drop."

Tension choking the room eased and Julia knew they'd avoided something pretty awful. At least for now. "We could use food and a good night's sleep."

Cam still didn't move. "Unless I need to worry about you calling the police the second I close my eyes."

"I'll agree not to call the police tonight if you agree not to run out into the rain with Julia," Sandy shot back.

She sighed at both of them...not that they were paying any attention to her. "I'm still right here."

Cam nodded. "Deal."

CAM HELD JULIA'S arms above her head and pushed into her one last time. Her head dropped back into the pillows, and her heels dug into the back of his legs. Watching her while she lost the last of her control was one of the sexiest things he'd ever seen.

She went wild, not holding back. Touching him, kissing him. And when her inner muscles grabbed on to him, his control snapped. His body bucked and the air rushed out of his lungs. Every muscle tightened until the last pulses moved through him. Then his bones turned to mush.

Desperate not to crush her, he rolled to the side and took her hand with him. Held it in his in the middle of his chest so they didn't break contact. He threw the other arm over his closed eyes and silently thanked Holt for handing him another condom back at the explosion scene. Cam had no idea how his friend knew, but he did. They didn't say a word. Just had a handoff.

Cam decided not to share that bit with Julia. She had enough on her mind without worrying about the team. She might not understand that the condom handoff meant acceptance. The Corcoran Team members were weird that way.

Cam's arm fell to the mattress. "I don't think this was what Sandy had in mind when he told us to go to bed."

"I'm a grown woman." Her legs shifted and a foot brushed up against his calf.

Cam wanted her to climb on top of him, but he'd need to build his strength back first. "No arguments here."

"I don't appreciate being talked about like I'm a child."

"Wait a second." At that tone, all surly and sharp, he lifted his head. "Am I in trouble for something?"

"Sandy is protective." She turned to her side and one arm snaked across Cam's stomach. "Overly so, and I don't always like the way he orders me around like I'm five."

Cam noticed, but he couldn't exactly get ticked off about the attitude. He had grabbed her in her father's house and dragged her into danger all over the island.

If the positions were reversed, Cam would have been skeptical. Might actually take out a gun and fire a shot to make sure she stayed safe.

The relationship with Sandy struck Cam as paternal. He knew she hadn't been close to her dad. She'd made that much clear. That could explain the tight hold on her. "Does he have kids?"

"Divorced a few times but no kids. He says he spent most of his younger business years making money and never at home."

"Now he's retired." Something about that fact caught in Cam's brain. A workaholic without a job, and Sandy was only about fifty.

"Which is weird." She rubbed her hand back and forth until her fingertips found Cam's exposed nipple. "He's not exactly the sit-around-the-house type."

Concentrating on the conversation became harder with each passing second, but Cam tried to stay engaged and ignore his resurging erection. He wanted to know about Sandy because something didn't feel quite right with the guy. "What does he do all day?"

"Count his money?"

"Me, too." Cam laughed at his own joke. "I think I have thirty-eight dollars."

"Dinner is on you when we get out of this." She stretched and her hand moved higher on his neck. Then she jerked and lifted herself up on her elbow. "Uh-oh. Did I scare you?"

He hadn't said anything, but his body went stiff. It was an involuntary reaction to the idea of commitment. His entire life had been about keeping free and being able to move. Except for the Corcoran Team, he'd never really believed in anything enough to commit to it.

He went with an answer that said nothing, because the idea of giving her the speech he'd delivered to others made him feel hollowed out inside. "I don't scare easily."

"But?"

Now was not the time. He had a prepared speech for this, but it clogged his throat and he couldn't figure out how to get it out. "You know I'm not the settle-down type, right? I go on missions and travel. I get shot at. A lot."

She leaned up on an elbow and stared down at him. "None of that is a surprise to me."

Nothing shook her. He'd never met a woman like her before, and the fact that he kept wanting to know more scared the crap out of him. "I'm just saying dating me is not easy."

She smiled. "Have you actually gone on dates? Like, at some point you found the time and strength to make it happen?"

Relief filled him at her amused tone. "Yes."

"And maybe one time in your life you've gone out with the same woman more than once?"

He wanted to laugh but went with an honest answer. "Yes."

"Do you see where I'm going with this?" She asked the question as if she were talking to a naughty child.

"You're telling me I'm overstating my dating issues."

"Yes." She slid over him, closing her eyes when the friction had them both groaning. "I'm not any different from the other women you've dated. You made it work with them, at least for a short time."

That was where she was wrong. That was the piece that had him both wanting to run and wanting to stay. "You're different."

She frowned at him. "Why?"

Cam thought about holding the truth back but let it fly. She'd earned his trust that much. "You matter."

"Well, that's pretty sexy." She leaned down and kissed his chin.

He moved his head to give her better access. "It's not a line."

She laughed and the sound vibrated through her. "That's what makes it so sexy."

Chapter Thirteen

Cam wandered through Sandy's house. He acted like a man who couldn't sleep, which was partially true. Julia had worn him out in the best possible way, but his mind kept churning. Something about this island, about the mystery surrounding Chief Kreider and the unanswered questions about Sandy, piqued Cam's innate need to investigate. Had his mind zipping away from Julia's warm body to something much more sinister.

The emergency call to Connor with Holt on the line didn't do anything to ease the concerns. Sandy had money but not the type Cam associated with this setup and the high-end, expensive security system that even Joel had trouble cracking. The situation made Cam wonder what the guy was hiding.

A workaholic who didn't work. Powerful and well-known in town. Had resources and was a hometown boy, so he knew every inch of the island. To Cam, eyeing Sandy made as much sense as checking out Chief Kreider.

One of those investigations would threaten what he had with Julia, even though he wasn't sure what that was. She talked about dating, and when she kissed him, every sensible promise he'd ever made to himself about stay-

ing unconnected and free while he did this job crashed
to his feet.

"You should leave."

At the sound of Sandy's voice, Cam turned around. It
wasn't a surprise that Sandy could sneak around without
making a noise. He seemed like the type, which was one
more reason Cam's alarm bells kept ringing. That and
the ninja security. Cam had spied two inside cameras—
one by the back door and one outside the closed office
door—and assumed they were recording every move.
It was the only reason he hadn't sneaked into the office
and looked around.

"I'm not going to hurt her." At least he was going to
do everything in his power to make sure no one else
touched her.

"Too late." Sandy kept walking until he stood in front
of the massive stone fireplace that divided the family
room from the sitting area on the other side. "She won't
say exactly how you two met, but if I had to guess I would
say you ran into her and then saw an opportunity."

Cam refused to lie about this point. If it ever came
down to criminal charges and him getting in trouble,
this bit of truth might save her from culpability. "You're
right."

"And you've been using her ever since."

That part he wouldn't cop to. "If you need to think so."

"Not even bothering to deny it?" Sandy shook his head
as he let out a harsh laugh. "I guess that's admirable."

"She was there. She knows what happened and what
I did." If the guy thought to blackmail or threaten, Cam
wanted him to know that tactic wouldn't work. He was
immune to that kind of pressure. "I didn't hide from her."

"But now she cares about you." Sandy leaned against

the armrest of the sprawling couch. "That makes her vulnerable and I don't want that for her."

Vulnerable was the last word Cam would use to describe Julia. She was, just like most people, but so many facets of her personality gave her strength that a very human vulnerability didn't weaken her at all in his eyes. "She's decent and compassionate."

"Interesting choice of description."

Sandy wasn't wrong. The words weren't strong enough, but Cam aimed for a different point. "She doesn't want me to get hurt while I figure out who's following us, which makes her a certain type of person. One I don't meet very often."

"We're saying the same thing."

Maybe they were. Cam wasn't sure, because Sandy lectured more than talked and getting to his point seemed to be a long journey. "I'm only here until I finish this assignment."

"I looked up the Corcoran Team." Sandy folded his arms across his chest. "You guys tend to get in the middle of a lot of trouble."

Not really possible. Except for a few cases, the group limited its internet presence and didn't advertise. Cases came to them through governments and corporations. Sometimes through connected individuals. But Connor worked miracles keeping the team and the members' individual names, as well as most of the details of their missions, out of the news.

Anything else would hamper their ability to move in and out and not be seen, which was usually how they operated. The bloodbath across Calapan was unusual and Cam knew Holt and Connor would demand explanations for every choice.

But it didn't hurt to see what Sandy did know. Possibly figure out how he knew it. Cam waded in. "Some people would say we solve trouble."

"They might," Sandy scoffed. "Not me."

The guy clamped down. It was as if he'd gone too far and showed his hand in admitting he'd checked the team out. Now he tried to pull back, all without showing one ounce of concern on his face.

Yeah, Cam didn't buy the caring-uncle routine for one second. This guy had skills and they came from somewhere.

"She'll forget you once you're gone, but you need to leave now while it's easier for her," Sandy said.

The comment sliced across Cam's senses. He hated every word and had to fight to keep his expression from changing. "She's an adult. She decides."

The last of Sandy's concern left his face. He stood up, looking ready to battle and much younger than fifty. "Be a man and do the right thing here."

Cam didn't even flinch. This guy did not scare him. And the fatherly advice rolled right off Cam. Maybe that was the one good part of never having one.

"We're leaving tomorrow morning." He didn't leave any room for question.

"You are." Sandy pointed toward the bedrooms. "She stays."

Now Cam saw it. The way Sandy stepped in and took over. Very paternal and borderline inappropriate even on the overprotective scale. "Does she know that? Julia does have a mind of her own and is old enough to make her own decision."

"She'll come to her senses."

Cam kept thinking the same thing. She'd wake up or

turn around and look at him and see what he saw when he looked in the mirror—a guy who did best on his own. "You can try to handle this however you want, but I'll let her decide."

"You'll see." Sandy nodded. "When the time comes she'll side with me."

JULIA ROLLED OVER and her hand hit a cool sheet instead of a warm male chest. She jackknifed into a sitting position and glanced around the room in time to see Cam walk back in from the hall.

"Why are you up?" She didn't bother whispering because she didn't think they had anything to hide.

Sandy had put them in two bedrooms. She'd vetoed that immediately and held her ground when he tried to explain that she needed sleep. She knew what she needed—Cam.

He jerked at the sound of her voice, then looked up at her. The frown came next. He made a face. Generally looked as though he was debating telling her the truth.

She knew then something bad had happened. "What?"

He hesitated for one more second before spitting it out. "The police are here."

She grabbed the sheet and held it to her chest. Until that moment she'd felt loose and comfortable, almost forgetting the horrors behind them and those yet in front of them. But the mention of police had her snapping back to reality.

Still, she didn't want to believe Sandy had betrayed her that way. "That's not possible."

"There's one police car outside. It's sitting at the end of the driveway."

Her heart crashed inside her chest. "You saw it?"

His expression stayed blank. "I'm guessing."

That didn't make any sense. She'd been with him non-stop and he didn't guess. He reasoned things out, listened to his team, researched the intel. Random guessing seemed odd…along with almost everything else that was happening on Calapan. "I don't understand."

Cam sat down on the side of the bed with his hand on the comforter covering her thigh. "Sandy wants me gone."

That was not news. She'd survived the earlier testosterone battle but knew that had only been round one. Looked as though they were at it again. "I'll talk to him."

"It's too late." Cam got up and went to the end of the bed. He had his jeans on and tucked in his T-shirt. "I need to sneak out."

"We are not having this discussion again. You go, I go." Even though the idea of getting out of that warm bed and stepping out into the wet dark night made her want to scream.

He froze in the act of putting a sweater on. "Julia, this is—"

"No, not again." She slipped over the usual arguments and zoomed right to the heart of what drove her. "I am sleeping with you because I care about you. Do you really think I'd let you wander off without me, especially if the police are looking to frame you?"

Cam dragged his sweater down his torso as his eyes grew soft. "Sandy will make sure no one hurts you."

"So will you." She stood up and moved to stand in front of him.

"No."

"I will follow you." Her hands went to his waist as she willed him to finally get it. She trusted him and would not leave him. "You know I will. Imagine the danger I can get into."

He sighed hard enough to blow her hair. "Get dressed."

She was already in her pants and searching for a shirt to go under his raincoat. By the time she stepped into the oversize bathroom a few minutes later, he stood there waiting by the alarm pad. Eyed it up and then looked to her.

The red light held steady. That meant the place was locked down, which made sense, as it was nighttime and normal people should be sleeping. She decided not to point that out and hoped she didn't fall asleep in the middle of their big escape.

She punched in the number on the keypad, but nothing happened. The alarm box beeped, but the light did not turn green. She tried again and got the same result, which made no sense.

She glanced over her shoulder at Cam. "The code isn't working."

"He changed it." Cam leaned back against the wall.

His comment made it sound as if Sandy had locked them in, but that couldn't be right. "Why?"

"He doesn't want us to get away this time."

Cam had broken into full-blown paranoia. She knew Sandy could be demanding and a whole host of other annoying things, but he didn't live in a prison and had never expected her to do so.

"What does that mean?" she asked. "You're being cryptic and now isn't the time."

"We need another way out. One that won't trip the alarms." Cam aimed his intense stare at her and did not let up. "Think."

"We can't just walk out, because the red light means the doors are locked and we'd need the override code."

"He has a system that locks him in? That's unbeliev-able." Cam shook his head. "Okay, any other ideas?"

The answer popped into her head immediately. "The balcony off his bedroom. He likes fresh air and keeps one of them open. He usually locks it out of the secu-rity system."

"This should be fun." Cam opened the door to the hallway just a fraction and looked out.

"We can take the back stairway, but he could be up there."

"I can't believe we're going up to go out." Cam went down on one knee in front of the duffel bag and loaded up with weapons.

Looked to her as if he planned on taking on an entire army before they broke free of the lawn. When the knife flashed and then disappeared by his side, her stomach rolled. "You're the one who insists we leave."

"And I'm right about that." He took her hand and brought her along behind him. "No talking."

As if she needed that warning. She thought all of this sounded overboard and odd, but the determination in his voice and on his face was not a joke. Neither was the sound of male voices coming from the front of the house.

Sandy was talking to…Kreider. Julia picked up the voice and double-timed the walk down the hall and around to the kitchen before the panic and confusion buzzing around her brain could catch up to her.

Cam pushed her back and out of the way when they got to the hallway that led to the foyer. If they could clear this they could get out without Kreider moving in. Never mind the fact that they'd have to rappel down the side of the house instead of just walking outside. She assumed Cam had a plan for that.

They waited. Stood there as Sandy talked about Cam being in the house and his concerns. Julia felt her temper build and boil, then explode in a flash before her eyes. Sandy had lied to her, and the reality of that burned through her, leaving her feeling raw.

One more peek and then Cam crossed to the other side in one giant yet quiet step. He held up a hand, keeping her back, then after a few seconds gestured for her to make a run. The plush carpet covered the noise of her footsteps and they stepped with caution as they walked upstairs.

She knew the floor creaked somewhere at the top of the steps and tried to circle around the general spot. But going into Sandy's bedroom for any reason felt weird. Not that she had a choice right now. Cam stood in the middle of the upstairs hall and held out his hands as if to ask for directions. She blocked out the violation and her anger at Sandy's bullying and moved toward the big double doors to the left.

Once she was inside, Cam frowned. She understood why. The bedroom was bigger than most houses and nicer than most hotel suites. It spanned almost half of this floor. The huge bed, still made, the sofa and desk. A wall of bookcases.

Cam hesitated at the desk. Brushed his fingertips over the handle to the top drawer but then shook his head.

She had no idea what was going through his head but guessed it had something to do with violating Sandy's privacy. She couldn't go there and snapped her fingers at him to let him know that.

With a nod Cam walked straight past her to the French doors to the balcony. One side was open and he slipped through. She could smell the rain and feel the breeze as it kicked up. They both stood at the railing and stared down the straight drop.

"Well?" She half mouthed and half whispered the word.

If he pulled a rope out of the pocket of his pants, she might lose it. But that wasn't what happened. He went to the bed and stripped it. The bedding rustled and the mattress bounced. Silk sheet slid over silk sheet with a strange, almost zipper-like, sound. Then he had them off and tied together and held them up as though he'd done a good thing.

She was pretty sure he'd lost his mind. "Are you kidding?"

He shrugged. "You can stay."

It was a dare and she refused to be baited. "Fine. You go first and wait for me to get down."

They went back out to the balcony and he dropped the makeshift rope. One end fell into the night and he secured the other to the marble column on the balcony. A tug and a pull and he looked ready to go.

"Hug the wall. Do not swing in front of the window." Cam glanced over the side. "I'll get down there and then hold it taut for you so it's easier to rappel."

"Fine." Except this was anything but fine. Growing up in Calapan with the mountains and steep trails heights didn't scare her. Falling to her death kind of did.

He slipped over the wall and was gone. No preparation or goodbyes. She was so fascinated watching the top of his head and the sure hand over hand as he scooted down that she almost missed the sound of footsteps echoing nearby. Her gaze shot to the closed door and she sensed she had only minutes to act.

She didn't wait for Cam to land. She pulled on the sheet and he looked up. Then she went over. He must have gotten the message, because he jumped the rest of the way and held the sheets steady for her.

She heard a sound above her head and a shout. The backyard flooded with light and for a second she stopped. Just hung there. With the plan imploding she did the only thing that made sense. She let go and closed her eyes, hoping Cam would have the sense and strength to catch her.

Her body jolted as it fell into his arms. One minute she snuggled up tight to his chest, and the next her feet hit the ground.

They took off running while male voices yelled from above.

She guided them around the patio furniture and pool, up the hill to the fence gate leading to the woods behind. The knob didn't move when she tried to turn it.

"Hold on." Cam lifted his foot and slammed his heel right by the lock.

The wood splintered and Cam kicked the pieces to the side. She didn't stop to ask questions. She ran until her chest ached and her throat burned. When she finally stopped she panted hard enough to bend her body over double.

Cam was right there with a hand on her lower back. Caressing, soothing.

He said something, but she ignored it to go with her own question as she glanced up. "Now what?"

He didn't hesitate. "The shipyard."

Chapter Fourteen

The sky turned a purplish pink right before the sun rose. The rain had stopped and the breeze died down, suggesting a normal summer day loomed before them. Cam welcomed some sense of calm, though he guessed it wouldn't last.

His gaze traveled to Julia where she sat on the trunk of a fallen tree. She tapped the toes of her shoes together and stared at the ground. Didn't make a sound as she tucked her hands between her thighs.

He knew the quiet wasn't a good sign. Julia liked to talk. Even through danger, she kept up a running commentary and asked questions. Now she sat stiff without making a sound, only rocking now and then.

"What do you know about Sandy's business?" He'd tried getting an answer several ways already without any real success. Any discussion on this topic seemed to shut her down. But he needed the intel, so this time he raced directly toward the point. "The actual source of his income and business."

Tap, tap, tap. "I already told you."

During the hike from Sandy's house, including the short-term borrowing of yet another car to get them most of the way to the shipyard area and the few hours of rest until morning, she'd shut down. He asked her about Sandy's money and his family and could see the wariness fall over her eyes. Instead of asking questions, she'd spent the drive staring out the window and offering directions in a flat tone.

She was smart enough to know why he was asking all about Sandy. Cam didn't have to explain. That didn't worry him. He wasn't looking to keep his concerns some big secret. But he didn't like the silence and lack of eye contact.

Cam tried again. "He's connected and wealthy and knows the island."

"That description fits a lot of people on Calapan."

He sat down next to her, hoping that closeness would help bridge the gap forming between them. "Then direct me to one of them. Tell me where to look and I'll have Connor and the rest of the team back in Annapolis start working."

When his leg touched hers, she shifted. "I don't live here anymore."

"Julia, come on." Cam inhaled, trying to wrestle the adrenaline pumping through him back under control. "I get that you're angry with me."

She slipped her hands out from between her legs and folded them on her lap. "I'm too busy trying not to be shot to be angry."

Could have fooled him. "I don't want Sandy to be involved."

She looked at him then. Slow and with a deliberate shift that highlighted that anger she claimed not to have, she stared at Cam. "You sure?"

Tension rolled off her and plowed into him. Gone was the soft woman from bed and the joking one from the trail. A certain seriousness had fallen over her and tightened her expression to the point of breaking.

This went beyond his questions about Sandy. Had to. The reaction was way out of proportion to his prodding. "What does that mean?"

Her head fell to the side, and her hair fell over her shoulder. "You don't like him."

There was no way for Cam to hide that, so he didn't try. Didn't hold back on his frustration, either. She actually sat there and accused him of getting an innocent man in trouble. "You think I'd set the guy up?"

She shrugged. "As you keep reminding me, I don't really know you that well."

Then it hit him. She was purposely picking a fight. The mix of exhaustion and frustration and feeling out of control had crept up on her and she'd come out fighting. He got it because he did the same thing now and then. But thinking he knew what was going on inside her and accepting being on the receiving end were two different things. She wasn't the only one looking for a way to control the situation.

Instead of yelling or reasoning with her, he stated a fact. "You're determined to be ticked off."

She stood up and whipped around to face him. The red stain on her cheeks suggested the anger had blown up on her. "He helped raise me. When my father was too drunk or too uninterested, Sandy stepped up."

"I get that."

"He was there for me. I know you don't get what that's like because of your upbringing, but he was."

The verbal shot landed right to his gut, and the last hold on his control broke. "Which explains why you came to the island and didn't bother to tell him."

As soon as Cam said the words he regretted them. She didn't do this work. It made sense for her to feel ripped apart and shredded. He didn't have an excuse.

When he started to talk she held up a hand to cut him off. "Stop talking."

"I overstepped." That qualified as a vast understatement, but right now it was all he could offer. After they solved the drug issue and got her to safety, he'd hold her and apologize and try to fix the part of the damage he'd inflicted.

Fury continued to vibrate off her, and those eyes stayed wild. She backed away from him and kept going until she moved right out of touching range.

"He was the first man I truly trusted," she said in a shaky voice.

The look, the pain all cut into him and he had to sit there and take them. "Julia, I—"

"Him, then you."

Her words hung there. The import of what she meant hit him a second later. That hollowed-out feeling in his chest came back and his mind blanked as he searched for the right words to say.

"Lovers' quarrel?" A man stepped out from the ruin off to their left of the half wall of what used to be a building. He held a gun and walked quickly as he moved right toward Julia. "That's a shame."

Cam reached out to grab her, but the effort came too late. In her need to get away from him she'd strayed a bit too far and the attacker, some guy Cam had never seen before, nabbed her first. He had his arm wrapped around her throat as he dragged her a few more feet away with a gun pointed at her head.

"This isn't your business." Cam stood up and closed

the gap between them. He had guns at his side and back and ankle. A few more knives rounded out his weapons inventory.

"You're on my property." The man dropped that verbal bomb without offering more.

Cam didn't believe it for a second. This guy had *underling* written all over him. He followed orders. He'd just happened to be lucky enough to stumble across them.

But Cam needed to confirm. "You own a shipyard?"

"My boss does."

Julia grasped at the arm confining her. Fingernails dug into the guy's jacket as her feet scraped against the ground. The guy had her in a headlock that almost lifted her off the ground and her panic filled the air.

Cam couldn't look at her. Couldn't see the pleading in her eyes. Not if he wanted to get through the next few minutes.

He pitched his voice lower and struggled to keep it even. "Then go get him and we'll work this out."

"Nice try, Mr. Roth."

Julia let out a soft sound and the attacker put his cheek against hers. "Yes, I know who you are, and you two have some lives to answer for."

She pushed the arm lower and lifted her head. "It was self-defense."

Cam didn't want her talking or moving. She needed to stay still while he stalled for an opening.

"I'm doing you a favor. You sounded pretty angry with your boyfriend, and now I'll get rid of him for you." The attacker laughed. "Then you can thank me."

She inhaled loudly enough to fill the quiet space. "No."

The attacker looked back at Cam. "Weapons on the ground or I start cutting her."

That was not going to happen. Not to her and not all of his weapons. Cam pulled out the gun on his side and held it up so both hands were in the air. "Let's stay calm."

"On the ground." The attacker used his chin to gesture toward Cam's gun. "Do it now."

She tightened her hold on the guy's arm. "Cam—"

He looked at her then. Focused all his attention on her and tried to send the silent message to hang on. "You're going to be fine."

And she would be. He'd promised her and that was back when she was an innocent woman he'd dragged with him on the run. Now she was more, so much more.

"You shouldn't lie to your woman." The attacker turned his head to look at Julia's face. "But maybe you won't mind seeing your boyfriend die."

Cam could see her hands shake and the disgust when she closed her eyes and tried to turn and put some room between her body and the man holding her. Terror or something close moved through her.

Cam could see it and wanted her attacker's focus back on him. "What's the next play here?"

"I have the authority to kill you." The attacker said the phrase with all the enthusiasm some people used to order breakfast.

Cam suspected that was true. He amounted to a nuisance, but he could be valuable and now he had to convince this guy of that fact. "But you should take me in."

"You don't make the rules."

"You don't, either." Cam took another step. "That's the problem, right? Men are ordering you around and you're sick of it."

"Be quiet." The guy snapped out the order as he jerked the arm holding Julia.

She choked and stumbled but stayed on her feet. When Cam took a step forward she waved off the concern. "I'm okay."

"For now." The attacker gestured for Cam to move. "Walk."

He'd done a quick look around when they got there. Hadn't seen footprints or signs of life. He had no idea if he'd missed something. "Where?"

"Through there." He used the gun to point to the doorway near the ruin where he'd appeared earlier. "And remember I have a knife to her throat, so don't try anything."

The guy was so busy talking and pointing that he created opportunities. Just what Cam expected from an amateur.

He waited for the next break in eye contact to drop his hands and slip the gun out of his waistband and into the pocket away from the attacker, then lifted them again. "I don't want her hurt."

"Hear that? You're in here cackling at him and he's trying to protect you." The attacker pulled her back against him. "Nothing to say?"

Fury burned through Cam and he almost went for his nearest weapon. "Don't touch her."

"You don't make the rules."

"I will lunge for you and make it hurt." Cam delivered the promise. "Snap your neck."

Something that looked like worry passed through the attacker's eyes before he nodded toward the entryway again. "Move."

Cam memorized every step and every piece of grass as he walked. The attacker took them through the ruins of one building, down a long grassy area to a small hill.

From there Cam could see the water beyond. Caught the scent of fish.

Between them and the shoreline were rusted-out carcasses of old ships and a series of buildings, most of them missing walls or a roof or both. One long narrow building looked mostly intact except for the blown-out windows and graffiti splattered over every smooth surface.

And the trucks. Two of them, both with their back doors open. There weren't any people working or moving around, but boxes littered the ground in front of the delivery vehicles as if this was the stuff left over after loading the good stuff. Made sense, since the bodies found around the island had drawn the attention of the media and law enforcement. Running the drug operation out of here—and suddenly Cam knew this was the right location—would be too risky right now.

Cam started down the slope. He made sure to keep his body as even with the attacker as possible. Out in front the guy might see the weapons, and Cam needed those.

The wet grass had his shoes slipping. The attacker had it harder, as he had to balance two people. Cam didn't help, because he was counting on a fall. When they got more than halfway down without incident, Cam started to rethink his strategy.

He glanced over at Julia. The attacker had her body bumping against his as her feet slid and ankles turned underneath her. Cam wondered about her injury and was about to look away to scan the area when she met his stare. Intense and determined, she glared as if willing him to understand, then her attention went to her feet. She repeated the action two more times.

A signal. He wasn't 100 percent sure of her plan, but he knew it included a fall. He answered with a short nod as the hand farthest away from the attacker dipped. He knew he'd have to grab and turn and shoot and do it all while gravity dragged him down the hill. Not the most convenient shot, but Julia had planned this, which meant she intended to duck and roll.

Good woman.

She took one more step and then her ankle turned. This time her knees buckled and her weight pulled the attacker down. He tried to catch her, but she was slipping and Cam was moving. The second she cleared the attacker's torso, Cam jumped over her body and slammed into the man, throwing him to the ground.

The man tumbled backward and momentum took Cam flying with him. They somersaulted and Cam lost hold of his gun. They rolled as he punched. He made a grab for the grass but couldn't stop the free fall.

They spun and when they landed the attacker ended up on top and took advantage. He punched Cam in the side, then did it again. Cam bucked his hips and the guy lost his balance. Cam slammed the guy into the ground on his side, then did a frantic visual search for his gun. Any gun.

An elbow crashed into his jaw, and his head shot back. Cam would've sworn he saw stars, but he blinked them out. He had to stay conscious. Had to win this one.

He saw a gun in the grass right in front of them as the attacker started crawling for it. Cam reached for the one by his ankle. Had it out and was about to aim when legs came into view. Julia's legs.

She stood just out of reach and held a gun. Had it pointed at the attacker's head. "I dare you to move."

The guy froze and looked up. He looked ready to go

for her legs when Cam shoved his weapon into the back of the guy's skull. "You heard her."

"It's tempting to tie something around his neck so he knows how it feels." Julia's chest rose and fell and her words came out choppy and disconnected, but the gun made her point.

Cam scrambled to his feet and put a heel in the middle of the guy's back before he could lift himself up. "You upset the lady."

He spit into the grass by her shoe. "Like I care."

Cam wrenched the guy's arms behind his back and held them with one of the last two zip ties he had in his pants pocket. Then he leaned down to make sure the guy could hear him. "You should, because now it's my turn to threaten you."

Chapter Fifteen

Julia leaned against what was once a wall of some building and rubbed her neck. She couldn't get the sick feel of this guy's beefy hands out of her head. The smell of his sweat and the sense of fear that wound around him and her. It all rushed back on her until she had to look away.

Even though he sat in a chair with his arms tied behind his back and one leg fastened to the chair, she waited for him to jump up and grab her again. She knew it was crazy and that Cam would shoot the guy first, but still.

Cam.

She'd pushed and picked at him because he'd targeted the one piece of her childhood that had always felt safe—Sandy. She believed in him and she believed in Cam and in one swift move Cam was trying to rob her of all of that.

"What's your name?" Cam stood in front of the attacker with both a gun and a knife in his hands.

The question had her attention zipping back to him. Despite the trickle of blood by his hairline, he looked totally in control.

He'd picked this building because it had walls and some protection, or so he'd said. It probably once consisted of workers' stations lining the long rectangular space. Now the plants had moved in. They grew up the walls and through the broken windowpanes. Grass sprinkled where the floor should be.

The entire place had a spooky, abandoned feel to it. This close to the water she could hear the waves splash. Every now and then a loud creak from the shift of some piece of metal out there in the ship graveyard would break the stillness.

She wanted to leave, but the attacker was not making that easy.

He shook his head and spit for what seemed like the fifth time. "I'm not saying anything."

"This is an easy one." Cam pocketed his gun but kept the knife out. "The questions will get harder."

She pushed off from the wall and joined them. Cam had contacted his team and they were on the way. The attacker couldn't know that. The watch Cam wore looked like any other dive watch, but it kept a line of communication open with Holt and Shane that just might save them all.

She stared down at the man who had terrified her enough a few minutes ago to steal her ability to speak. "Tell him."

"Shut up," the guy shot back.

"Hey." Cam smacked the guy in the side of the head. "You don't get to talk to her like that."

The attacker's gaze switched from Cam to her. "So the fight was a fake. You were pretending to be ticked off." He shook his head. "I should have known from the topic. A dumb thing to fight over."

Well, that was embarrassing. She cleared her throat to let Cam know she planned to chime in before he could. "Yeah."

The attacker's gaze switched to Cam. "Who are you?

I know your name, but what or who has you killing men across the island?"

"I'm someone you should listen to." Cam managed to look and sound bored. "Your name. Now."

"Ned."

Julia wasn't sure what good knowing did. She actually didn't want him to have a name. That way she could think of him as a nameless attacker and not an actual person.

Cam played with his knife. Looked as though he wasn't even interested in anything Ned did or said. "Okay, Ned. Tell me about Ray Miner."

Ned frowned. "How do you—"

"You should assume I have access to information, weapons and resources." Cam grabbed the only other intact chair and put it in front of Ned. "Ray Miner."

"Second to the boss."

A wave of excitement hit Julia. The guy kept coughing up information. The more they collected, the closer Cam would get to solving the case. And then he'd leave... That burst of excitement fizzled out as quickly as it came.

Cam put one foot on the seat of the chair. It wobbled but didn't disintegrate. "Who is the boss?"

"I don't know."

Cam didn't even blink as he balanced his arm on his knee and leaned in closer to the guy. "Try again."

"You can ask it a hundred times and the answer will be the same." The blade flashed and a line with bubbles of blood showed up on Ned's cheek, causing him to duck his head and flinch. "Ouch."

Cam let out a long sigh. "It only gets more painful from here."

She hadn't seen this side of him since those first couple minutes after he stormed into her dad's house.

Controlled with a deadly calm to his voice. He showed off his weapons, and everything about the way he held his body suggested he would use them.

Ned must have felt the power shift, too, because he started talking. "I dealt with Ray. He hired me."

"Where is he now?" Cam asked.

"Here." Ned looked around, moved his head from side to side.

Her heart slammed to a stop. "What?"

The question brought Ned's attention to her. He no longer looked angry. If anything he seemed pleased with himself. Certainly not scared. "He's on the grounds somewhere."

Cam didn't let up. His intensity still held the room captive. "What's happening at the shipyard?"

Julia found herself leaning in. This was the question she wanted answered. After years of nothing happening here, of all the decay and loss, it sounded as if someone had stepped in and opened a business. Drugs instead of ships, a terrible exchange.

Ned broke eye contact to stare at the floor. "I'm done talking."

She didn't know if it was guilt or his way of taking responsibility, but she wanted everything clear. If he wouldn't say the word, she would. "Drugs."

Cam smiled as he shot her a quick glance. "He thinks we don't know."

Ned's head shot up. "You're guessing."

"Wrong." Cam made a show of exhaling as he dropped his foot and moved the chair out of the zone between them. "You're supplying a new hybrid drug that has the nasty side effect of stopping some people's hearts."

The information screeched through Julia's brain. She

knew about the witness…poor Rudy. But Cam knew more details. He'd had a specific assignment—come to the island, talk to the police chief, then go fetch a witness, who happened to be Rudy. But now and then he'd let some other detail slip, which made her wonder what else he knew but wasn't saying.

As soon as the thought moved through her head, she saw Sandy's face. Now Cam had her doubting a man she always trusted.

"People shouldn't use drugs if they can't handle them." Ned delivered that gem.

He wasn't wrong, but hearing life advice from him made Julia's back teeth slam together.

"You have law enforcement on edge from Canada down to Mexico," Cam said.

Ned answered that with a feral smile. "Which should tell you about the power you're dealing with here."

"Whatever." Cam didn't look or sound impressed. "Where are the drugs?"

"Not talking."

She grew weary of running into wall after wall. They'd make progress and then lose ground. All she wanted was a firm mattress and a few hours rolling around in the sheets with Cam. They could talk and argue and anything else he wanted so long as they broke free of the mess that had bogged them down for days.

And this guy was the perfect place to start. "Your boss is going to think you talked, so you may as well cough up something and make it easier on yourself."

Cam shrugged. "She's right."

"He won't believe you." Ned said the right words, but his tone didn't match. Didn't sound sure.

"I am very persuasive." Cam brought the blade in front of Ned's face. "You want me to show you?"

"You won't—"

"Watch me." Cam held the knife right there. "See, you touched her and no one touches her without her permission."

She smiled at that. To think she ever doubted him.

RAY LOWERED THE rifle and watched Ned's face. From his position a solid three hundred yards away, Ray could see his targets walking around and his man sitting. He guessed they were having a conversation and that it wasn't a willing one on Ned's part.

The guy deserved it. Ray had watched Cam grab the advantage. He'd gotten the drop on Ned with the woman's help. It was an embarrassment for someone paid as well as Ned was. So was the fact that they all now sat there, chatting like old friends.

The talking was the problem. Sharing information couldn't happen. Ned knew about pieces of the operation and how they had started loading up trucks yesterday thanks to the news of incoming law enforcement to investigate all the murders. He didn't make the product, but he understood what it was and how lucrative it had turned out to be.

Ray had known Cameron Roth was on his way to the island to talk with someone. Enter Rudy, a onetime decent employee turned scared. Ray got to Rudy just in time and got him to crack. Killing him after actually came as a relief.

That had left the task of erasing the concerns Rudy had raised. Ray had arranged to play the role of police chief and stall Cameron's meeting with Rudy since the guy was already dead anyway. Ray's men handled the fake witness handoff.

The original plan had been to step in and eliminate Cameron before he caused trouble. To limit the disruption in production while they set him up and cleared the slate. But Cameron must have sensed trouble. First came the gunfire, then Cameron took off. And that woman kept popping up. The combination had the plan quickly falling apart.

The explanations to the boss all fell to Ray. Bigger for him, Cameron and his crew had ruined Ray's plans to make a move on the business. But overtaking anyone now that the equipment and crew were spread out and set to start leaving the island in shifts would be impossible. Ray had to wait. Double back and let the business reset before he moved in.

But he could kill Cameron Roth now. Just for fun.

Ray lifted his rifle to do just that. Would have blown the guy away, but he had company. Two men walked up. Since Roth didn't panic and the woman's body language suggested she was pleased, Ray assumed this was the rest of the group. These were the men of the Corcoran Team, at least the ones in town. If Ray wanted to go after the others, he'd have to travel to do it.

Tempting.

Now they had a squad of people to ask questions of. People everywhere who could pull details out of Ned and then put them together in a coherent way. Ned might not have all the pieces, but this team had the ability to bridge some of the mental gaps.

That left one choice. Not the one he wanted to make, but the right one.

It wasn't that he cared all that much for Ned, because

he didn't. The guy laughed at the wrong times and always seemed to be a step behind when talking tactics. But he could shoot and his size intimidated, so not having him on the payroll would be a loss.

Ray raised his rifle again. While it was tempting to unload and shoot them all, the problem of keeping the woman alive still lingered. The boss was already furious about having his trade interrupted. Having a stray bullet nick the one person he wanted alive in this thing would borrow trouble, and for now Ray was not the boss.

He looked again. Using the well of patience he kept for this sort of situation, he aimed. Lay there and watched. When the people cleared out of the way, he sighted on Ned's forehead…and fired.

Chapter Sixteen

Holt and Shane arrived before Cam could use the knife. Probably a good thing. Cam turned to welcome them to the strange party just as he heard the crack. The constant stream of noise around the shipyard as the place settled muffled the sound. The building creaked and groaned but somehow stayed up. But this was different. More focused and familiar.

He jumped in front of Julia. Thought about bringing her to the ground so he could cover her but stopped when she dived into his chest and cuddled there. Wrapping around her, he got her to the wall so her back would be protected by the wall while his body took care of the front.

Holt and Shane must have heard the sound, too, because they both turned and dropped. Holt headed for the wall directly across from Cam. The lack of furniture and firm structure made it hard to take cover. The few desks and random chairs bordered on sawdust thanks to the exposure to the elements and lack of use. Not exactly the best shields.

"That was—" Then Cam saw it. The noise had been a shot. No mistake about that now. And someone with some skill had fired it, because it'd connected to its target. "Damn."

Julia lifted her head. "What?"

Holt was the one to swear this time. He let out a string, then dropped to his knees next to Ned's body. The man's head tipped forward and blood dripped from somewhere. When Holt moved it back, Ned's eyes were closed. The only true sign of trouble was the tiny hole marring his forehead.

Cam moved Julia then. He hustled her over next to an old heater. When he ducked he brought her with him. Tucked her in front of him, tight against the wall. She mumbled something, but he couldn't hear her as Shane and Holt scurried around for better cover.

It took another few seconds to realize that in the chaos only one shot had sounded. Yeah, there could be more. The shooter could be waiting and excited to take them out one by one.

The mumbling near the side of his head finally caught his attention. He leaned in until Julia's mouth tickled his ear.

"What did you say?" he asked her.

He expected her to scream or confirm her hatred for Calapan. Both seemed fair to him at the moment. Instead, she whispered one word against the tip of his ear. "Sorry."

At first the sentiment didn't compute. She'd been both a good sport and a huge help just about from the first time they met. Her ability to stay calm in the face of terror amazed him. Which made her flat comment and dead eyes even more of a concern.

He lowered his head so only she could hear. "For what?"

"Doubting you."

The Sandy thing.

Cam knew that would come up again. That they'd churn through that topic a few times before coming to any sort of agreement.

And, man, he wanted to kiss her. Right here in the middle of danger and in front of his team. That was what she did to him. Took all of his caution and blew it away. Replaced his common sense with a blinding need for her.

No question hearing her wonder earlier about his motivations had dug into him. He was equally sure that her moment of uncertainty made sense. Sandy had been in her life forever. Cam had been in it for about forty-eight hours. Even for people without trust issues, blind faith was a rough call.

Cam saw Holt stand up and Shane unfold his body from where he'd slipped in behind Ned's chair and waited. Cam watched each move, knowing there was so much more for them to get through this morning, including knocking out a random shooter.

But he needed her to know one thing first. "You were great."

She glanced up then. "I was angry."

"That looks hot on you."

"Cam." Holt's voice carried across the open space. "This guy is out of the picture. Nothing more we can get from him."

Which was a shame. Cam truly believed Ned would have coughed up some more details. He wasn't the loyal type that rode his information to the grave. He would have been a good but reluctant source of intel.

That was probably an excuse for why he was no longer breathing. The guy couldn't be a threat if he didn't open his mouth. "Someone didn't want him to talk."

Holt looked at Julia and she froze. "Should I know who?" she asked.

Shane didn't wait for an answer to that one. "Did he say anything valuable?"

"Confirmed the drug operation and Ray Miner's role but didn't know anyone above Ray, only that someone was." That grated against Cam's nerves. The men were out here producing and transporting. On an island and away from everyone else. He didn't understand how the boss kept his identity a secret.

The success made Cam think Ned might have actually met the man in charge and didn't know it. If the guy who ran the operation was connected and well-known, which they all seemed to agree on, he'd have to be careful as he moved around.

Holt stood with the binoculars in his hands and looked into the open greenery, following what he thought was the trajectory of the shot. "I'm thinking whoever he is can shoot a gun with pretty good accuracy."

"I doubt the boss does any of the dirty work," Shane said.

"Then it should be easy to flush him out." Cam agreed, but they felt so close to figuring out this conspiracy that he wanted it disbanded and the members spread in different jails. "Create a problem and have him come running."

"A problem like how we keep killing his men?" Julia asked in an amused voice.

Cam settled on one point—she'd said *we*, and he believed she actually viewed the situation that way. She put her body in as a team member's.

He didn't hate that comparison.

"Why are you walking around?" Julia hadn't left her

safe spot next to the wall. She stood there, anchored and not moving. "The shooter could still be up there."

Shane shook his head. "He's long gone."

"How do you know that?" She glanced up at the spot where Holt had just been looking. "He could be waiting, just like he's been doing all day."

Cam knew the answer to that, but he wasn't sure telling her would ease her worry. He debated. Went back and forth and then spelled it out. "He wanted Ned here."

"If he wanted the rest of us, we'd be dead." Shane took a second to go over to her. He patted her shoulder, and from the way she flinched after each pat, Cam guessed Shane wasn't clear on how much force he used.

"Is that supposed to be comforting?" She rubbed the spot where he'd knocked against her with his palm.

Cam thought she was probably talking about the words and not the awkward bonding moment. "Poor Shane."

"No kidding," Holt whispered.

She left the sanctuary of the wall and joined them closer to the middle of the room, or warehouse floor or whatever it was. "It's scary to me that you're the best with people of the three of you."

"We used to have a fourth team member. A woman." Cam smiled when he thought about Erica. She'd been recently divorced and a sharpshooter. She could nail a target from distances that left others gawking. "She played the role of human-emotion interpreter."

Julia tried to ask a question and stumbled. She got it out the second time. "What happened to her?"

The confusion made sense. A lot of times people didn't think about women being lethal. Erica was, even though she looked as if she made a fortune in tips tending bar.

"Assignment with a bodyguard agency. She loves it, so I'm thinking we've lost her forever."

"Then I'll take over the female role." Julia pulled up straight and stared them all down. "For now."

Holt glanced over at Shane. "She's bossy."

Cam nodded. "I still like it."

"I'm thinking the only person she cares about here is Cam," Holt added.

"Enough." Cam seriously considered banging their heads together. "She is in the room and capable of talking."

Julia saved her smile for Holt and Shane. "You two are growing on me."

RAY LOOKED AT the message on his phone. It wasn't like the boss to leave a trail of any sort. Not that any phone they used could trace back to the guy. He was careful and he knew how traces worked. No way would he let something as simple as a phone trip him up.

But the words crawled across the screen and Ray could not ignore them. He had to drive out past that falling-down farmhouse and all the outbuildings on the ship-yard property. He'd cleared the men out in an attempt to restore the shipyard and not raise questions. Some of the men carried loads on trucks and had coordinates for safe houses.

Everything had been split up so no one would benefit by going rogue and trying to smuggle the contents out on their own. Not that they could or that the boss would tolerate the loss anyway. All anyone had to do was ask Rudy. The boss demanded loyalty and got it.

And what the boss wanted mattered...for now. Because according to his message, he'd be there in a few minutes and he had a plan.

Chapter Seventeen

They all stood around while Holt and Connor, the one she'd never met and still only saw via a tiny screen, had some sort of virtual meeting. They talked facial recognition and drugs and something about trucks. Julia had trouble keeping up because she could barely hold her eyes open.

The danger hadn't passed, but it sounded as if the drugs were on the move, which should mean the people connected to the drugs were looking for a way out. That seemed like good news to her, even though the Corcoran guys looked ticked off that they couldn't capture someone to take to the police.

She balanced her hands behind her on what used to be a windowsill and watched Cam approach. That sure walk was back in place and his newest round of aches and bruises had been cleaned up in about two seconds by Shane. She guessed injuries suggested weakness, so these guys willed the pain away.

"Hey." That was all she had left. A simple greeting. Not even a full sentence.

Cam stood next to her and scanned the room as Shane and Holt moved around, with Shane taking photos and Holt talking to his watch.

For some reason none of it struck her as weird. Shooting, killing and chitchatting via watch seemed normal. The fact that people out there still wanted Cam dead and her captured didn't even register anymore.

Cam pressed in close enough for his body to touch hers from arm to thigh. "Any chance I can talk you into taking one of those ferries today?"

He just kept playing this refrain. Each time it got a little more tempting to say yes and demand he go with her. She was on a leave of absence and had a little time left, but this wasn't exactly her idea of a vacation. "Are they running?"

Cam crossed one ankle over the other and continued to stand there. "Connor is working on it."

She looked at Cam and saw competence. She'd heard about Connor and wondered if the guy was even human. He seemed to be able to pull off any errand or favor. He might be the leader of the team, but it sounded more as though he should lead the country.

"I have to meet your big boss." Though she'd be tempted to give him a bill for all the therapy she feared she'd need in the future thanks to this operation of his.

"You'd like him." Cam smiled. "You'd probably like his wife even more."

His...wife... "He's married?"

Cam winced. "Yeah."

For some reason that information stopped her. After the "no commitments" lecture from Cam and the lack of rings on Shane and Holt, she'd assumed the whole team had a hands-off policy. The reference to a wife blew that idea.

"I guess that means *he* found time to date at some point." And only Cam hid behind that crazy excuse.

She was joking, but the thought of that and his pledge and his strange insistence that going out with him could only be a one-off thing started an ache in the center of her chest.

He closed one eye as if he were thinking of the comment only. "I'm impressed with your ability to fall back on an argument from earlier as if we never finished that conversation."

"And win it in a landslide." She wanted that clear. She made her point and kept making it.

He nodded. "That, too."

She thought about picking at that topic a little more. She could demand an answer about the next time they saw each other, ensuring that there would be a next time. When the idea of something happening between them past tomorrow rose, he panicked. Got all twitchy and started shifting around. It was cute...and a little insulting. Here she was, so in tune to him that she could sense his moods, and he dwelled in this fear that she would start demanding things.

Looked as though she was not the only one with a trust issue.

Wading through the personal, she went right to the workday stuff. "What happens now?"

"Connor called in law enforcement. Some are on the way to the island and others have arrived but are stationed at the ferry, watching the docks and any way on and off the island by water. Ray thinks he has control of the boats, but he doesn't. If those trucks move, we should get them."

She tried to imagine how the privacy-protecting citizens of Calapan would take being infiltrated by law-enforcement types. Then a bigger question popped into her mind. "Are these law-enforcement folks going to make the murder charges against you go away?"

"Unless I tick off Connor."

She laughed then and all three of the men stared at her. "So probably not, then."

"Call is almost over." Shane walked up, already talking. "Connor is searching for more information on Ned."

"How does that help?" she asked because she honestly didn't know. The guy was dead and for her that ended the line of questioning. But what did she know?

"If we know about him, we might be able to find a string and trace it back to the leader of this drug show." Shane didn't name a name or tag Sandy as a possible suspect. He just laid the facts out and then walked away.

Not the chattiest guy she'd ever met.

She leaned into Cam. When he didn't push back or show any signs of feeling uncomfortable with the innocuous touching, she put her head on his shoulder. "Your job is exhausting."

"We rest eventually."

Shane spun around and stared at Cam. "Heads up. We have company."

"How does he know that?" The guy had just been standing there.

"He's spooky like that." Cam stood up and took her along with him. "Who?"

No one answered, but the room seemed to spin with sudden motion. They could scatter, but it would be too easy for someone to see them and follow the weakest link, which she feared was her.

Cam, Holt and Shane all stood with weapons. They formed a barricade of sorts by standing in a line. To her that made them targets, and none of them raced around to hide. But they did stand in front of her. She had to go up on tiptoes to see what was happening in front of her.

Cam's voice broke into the quiet. "We need to find better assignments from now on. Stick the Annapolis guys with the drug stuff."

A second later Chief Kreider showed up at the far end of the long room. He held a gun but didn't have any men with him. None that she could see, but they could just be off waiting somewhere. Totally possible and a little creepy.

"You can start thinking about that new job right now." Kreider aimed his weapon at Cam, clearly ignoring the fact that he was outnumbered by a decent margin. "Hands in the air. All of you."

None of them moved. Julia looked around and Holt and Cam wore similar expressions of disbelief. Shane whistled. Actually whistled. They didn't appear ruffled or impressed with Kreider's big show. She didn't like the guy either, but a gun was a gun.

"Maybe we should all stay calm." That applied to her as much as them, but she felt the need to say it.

The chief didn't take his eyes off Cam. "Ms. White, you are in no position to demand anything, but you would be wise to step on out here and come to me."

Cam's arm shot out. "No. She stays with me. Always."

Something about the way he said it had those nerves jumping around in her stomach calming just a bit. The urge to run and throw up still tried to overtake her, but she beat it back and focused on Kreider. The man hadn't changed in years. Still grumpy and demanding and generally hating women.

"Tell your friends to drop their weapons and get on

the ground or I will open fire." Kreider talked to her as if they got along.

She couldn't think of one time when he'd sided with her or helped her. He was too busy protecting his old friends to actually do anything to keep Calapan a place where people would want to live. The drug issue was only the example of his inability to do his job.

Holt frowned. "No one is threatening you. What would justify the use of force against any of us?"

"The dead men all over Calapan Island."

She had to admit Kreider had a point. Even if he wasn't guilty on the drug charge—and she was not ready to say that yet—he couldn't let Rudy's death and those of the others pass without any discussion.

But for a man who had supposedly been tracking them for days, it sure had taken him a long time to find them. Made her wonder why now. "Why are you here?"

Kreider barely spared her a glance. "You're not the one asking questions."

"What about me?" A strong male voice echoed down the other end of the room.

Another man in uniform walked into the building from the opposite end. They were surrounded by law enforcement, even though this second one wasn't real. He hadn't been real police when he shot at Cam and chased him to her father's house. Hadn't been real police when he brought two of his goons into Dad's house and scared her.

"Ray Miner. You and Chief Kreider are quite the pair." Cam made a face. "It's like the worst welcome party ever."

Kreider crowded in toward the still body in the chair, and the men parted to let him pass. Kreider did a check of the pulse, then called it in on his radio as a murder.

Never asked for backup or explained what was happening. An interesting choice for someone who was supposed to be keeping the whole town safe.

Then he turned back to Cam. "What a surprise, Roth. I find you and end up tripping over another dead body."

Cam nodded in Ray's direction. "And you brought a fake law-enforcement official to this unwanted meeting. Good call."

"Again with that argument." Kreider shook his head. "Miner here is legitimate. I called and checked his references myself."

"What did you use for verification? Because it's wrong," Shane said.

But Cam was already off and running. "You can't be this bad at your job. You just can't."

Every word sliced through her. The Corcoran men were tough and ready for almost anything, but their guns weren't up, and bad-mouthing a police officer was never a good idea. On the tiny island of Calapan it was really bad.

"Can we all put the weapons away and talk this over?" She hoped Cam would ignore the *all* part and keep one on him just in case.

"My weapons stay with me," Shane said.

"I don't think so." Ray approached Holt first. "Weapons on the floor or Ms. White will pay the price."

Cam glanced at Holt before returning his attention to Ray. "For the record, that doesn't make you sound legitimate even with the uniform."

She knew that look. There was a plan in motion. She didn't know what or how she could help, but she sensed motion coming.

She did what she could to stall for time. "Wouldn't just talking, without the weapons, be a better use of our time?"

Kreider ignored her and started his own conversation. "Why are you all here? This is private property."

"Are you afraid the corporation will get upset?" Cam asked.

Kreider frowned at him. "Last I checked, an individual owned the property."

She listened, fascinated, as the team picked up pieces of information without a full-on interrogation. Just went to prove that most people liked to pass on what they knew. They talked and shared and made a mess of everything.

"We came to town for a meeting with Rudy, who is now dead, but we know there is a drug problem here." Cam held out his arms. "That's why we're here. We needed to find the operation, and now we have."

"I checked the grounds and there's nothing here," Ray said.

Kreider looked up and down the room. "Yeah, Roth. You see something I don't?"

"It's mostly been cleaned out," she said.

She hated that part. After all they'd been through, it only seemed fair that they would get to the end of the chase and find a room full of something and be able to point to it as proof of her innocence.

Ray chuckled. "Convenient."

"Not really," Cam said as he folded his arms in front of him.

Something in the way he moved suggested Ray was getting twitchy. He widened his stance and pulled out a zip tie. "This is the last time we're telling you to get on the floor."

"Or?" Holt asked.

That tone. Those expressions. She was prepared to

dive out of the line of battle if it came to that. "Maybe if we went with fewer threats."

"Swab the walls and floor. Check the buildings and those trucks outside. You'll find the evidence of a drug lab." Cam's gaze did a quick bounce to Ray before coming back to settle on Kreider. "We have nothing to hide."

Ray shook his head. "I'm taking you all in, including the woman."

"Hold up." Kreider held out a hand. "They're mine."

"Actually, gentlemen—" Holt's husky voice cut through the arguing "—we're not going anywhere."

"I'm tired of this." Ray raised the gun and fired.

Kreider hit the floor and the team pulled their weapons. She was the only one without a gun in her hand, but she barely noticed. The shock of seeing the chief fall back, just wither and slide, echoed in her head.

By the time she looked up again, Ray had one gun on the men and one aimed at her. She shifted and the barrel followed.

Ray's smile turned feral. "Now are you all ready to listen?"

"You just killed your boss?" Cam asked.

"I think we can both agree I'll make a better boss." Ray kicked Kreider's foot. "I managed to trick him and most of this dumpy island into thinking I was a police officer."

"Why?" Julia wasn't even sure what question she was asking. Why do this, why the killing and the lying? Why use poor Calapan as his stomping grounds?

"I'm stronger, smarter. More efficient."

When he went with his ego she wasn't sure how to respond. She glanced at Cam and he shook his head. Slight but she saw it.

"So this was all you." Cam shifted his stance. The move put him closer to her. "The setup and production, all you?"

"Yes."

Cam's eyes narrowed. "Transportation and break-down."

Ray waved off the question. "We're done talking."

"It's four against one," Shane pointed out.

She liked those odds. She'd seen what Cam could do when he was on the one side, and she thought this had to be better.

"Not really because, first, I'm not alone." Ray continued to aim a gun at her. "And second, anyone comes near me or if I feel even a twinge from a muscle cramp, I will assume you are at fault and punish the woman."

The whole feeling-better thing gave way to waves of nausea. "Why do you want me?"

"I'm going to have to insist you all disarm...unless you want to hear her scream."

Cam held up his hands. "Fine. You win this round."

"What are you doing?" The shock came through in Shane's voice.

She wondered the same thing. There were three of them. Even if reinforcements lingered out on the property somewhere, these guys had the advantage.

Cam glanced at Shane. "I won't let him hurt her. We're fine without them."

"That's sweet." Ray waved his weapon. "All the guns. Now."

She heard a series of clicks and thuds as they took off the firepower. Holt and Cam wore three guns each. Shane unpacked for what felt like forever. By the time they were done, the area in front of them was littered with weapons.

"Come here." Ray pointed at her.

She didn't move, but Cam clamped a hand over her arm anyway. "She stays with me."

"I'm afraid not." Ray used the side of his foot to move the guns. Shifted them out of the direct reach of the Corcoran men. "You see, I have a need for her."

Her stomach flopped. "What does that mean?"

"You're useful." He reached for her. "Be grateful."

Everything happened so fast after that. She shrank back from his touch at the same time Shane kicked Ray in the hand. Bodies moved and she tried to keep track of Ray's gun, but she lost sight when Holt and Shane moved in.

She heard a yell akin to a battle cry. She wanted to close her eyes and hide, but she watched. Saw Cam let his knife fly and Ray squealed when it sliced through his shooting hand. The gun dropped and Shane jumped on it as Holt tackled Ray to the floor.

When the chaos calmed, Holt had Ray pinned, but he didn't notice. He was too busy rolling to his side as he cradled his hand.

Then Cam's face appeared in front of her. "Are you okay?"

She tried to draw enough air into her lungs to breathe. "That was the plan?"

Cam shot her a smile. "He only asked for the guns."

"And we wanted him alive." Holt stood and pulled Ray up beside him.

He was cursing and trying to roll into a ball. "You will all pay."

He sounded wild and out of control. His words slurred and the blood continued to flow. The guy needed medical help and a prison cell. She didn't think the order mattered.

While Holt and Shane dragged him out, she tried to reboot her brain. She felt raw and exposed and not prepared to do anything but slide to the floor in a heap.

Cam's arms came around her. "It's going to be okay."

She said the first thing that came into her mind. "I want to see Sandy."

Cam's shoulders stiffened, but he placed a gentle kiss in her hair. "Me, too."

Chapter Eighteen

Two hours later Ray was in the hospital with Holt by his side. He hadn't started talking, but it was only a matter of time. Finding the trucks took a little longer. Kreider or Ray or whoever had played that one smart, which ticked Cam off. Didn't try to remove the trucks from the island. Just hid them and waited.

No doubt about it, someone with smarts led this drug ring. Cam still didn't believe it was Kreider.

Sandy let the refrigerator door close and turned around to the counter with a water in each hand. He handed one to Julia and Cam took the other.

"Kreider's a drug dealer?" Sandy shook his head as he twisted off the cap to his bottle.

"Was." Julia shivered. "He's not anything now."

Cam slipped his hand over her leg and gave her knee a squeeze. She'd been thrown around and injured, so he almost hated to touch her. Except for the other part of him that was desperate to touch her.

Sandy continued as if she never spoke. "Either way, it doesn't really make sense."

Cam didn't think so, either. He sat on the bar stool in Sandy's kitchen and tried to make the pieces fit together, but they wouldn't. Nothing in Kreider's demeanor suggested he'd worked with Ray in the drug trade. Kreider had acted as if he thought the other man was a legitimate law-enforcement officer.

There was no evidence in Kreider's finances or history to support his being some drug kingpin. Even though he wasn't the greatest police chief, everyone agreed he worked long hours. He liked to hang out in his uniform and visit with people. That hardly left a lot of time to run up to the shipyard and oversee production.

And then there was the comment about the ownership of the shipyard now. Connor and Joel were working on that pile of shell companies and business names right now, but Cam thought he could find the answer in a much easier way. "Who purchased the shipyard from you?"

Sandy slowly lowered the water bottle. "Excuse me?"

"Julia told me a company bought it and then ran it into the ground." If they knew who, maybe they could trace the whole thing back to Kreider and put it to bed.

Until then, as far as Cam was concerned, the case was not over. Many of the people who could explain were dead. Kreider was supposed to be the boss, but no matter how many times Cam turned that over in his head he couldn't make sense of it.

Julia finished off the bottle and clunked the plastic container against the counter. "It was a Canadian outfit. I remember that much from my father's complaining."

Cam didn't want to go down that road and open up those memories again. She'd already made it clear she hadn't trusted her dad. Anything that raised his name or even for an instant made her tie him to her father was a no-go for Cam.

"Do you remember the name?" he asked Sandy.

"It doesn't matter, because it was sold again." Sandy

went back to the refrigerator. This time he pulled out a plate of food with foil over the top. "Hungry?"

The whole scene struck Cam as surreal. Julia was out of it, almost comatose. She'd been through threats and pain and shootings and fires. She needed to recuperate for more than a few hours to be back on track.

And Sandy didn't seem to care about any of it. A civic leader who didn't have a single reaction to the idea of drug runners taking over the business he had once nurtured and built. Not when he was hungry.

The ticking at the back of Cam's neck kicked up again. Nothing had felt right about this assignment since he walked onto the island. The supposed resolution of the case being the biggest question mark for him.

"I need to head over to the clinic." The words came out before Cam could even think them through.

She stopped in the middle of reaching over to steal his water bottle. "Why?"

"Ray Miner is awake and talking." In truth he was awake and staring at the ceiling. He insisted he was the boss and it was his operation now that Kreider was gone. He implicated the dead man and then clammed up.

It was too convenient. Though it didn't make much sense to Cam that a man with Ray's ego would take part of the fall for anyone else. It was possible his hubris drove him to claim more responsibility than he had. His personality might just not let him be seen as a simple employee. Either way, he was going to prison, which was a good thing for everyone.

"That's good, right?" Julia shook her head as the memories played across her face. "That guy should not be out among people."

Cam wanted to stay and comfort her. Guilt smacked

into him at the thought of opening this door with her one more time after she'd been so clear and so broken when he broached it before.

But Cam kept playing the role. If Ray really was the boss, no harm could come from this. But if he wasn't, this might draw the real boss out. "He's not happy with how things ended for him. Apparently he thought he should be the boss, and that bitterness should work for us."

Cam stared at Sandy until he finally piped up with a response. "Good."

"I'll go with you." Julia slid off the bar stool.

"You need to stay here and get some rest." He was deadly serious about this. There wouldn't be an argument or a battle. He was winning this round. If Sandy made a move on Ray, she should be here, out of the fray. "She injured her ankle."

Sandy frowned. "What?"

"It's fine."

Before she could downplay it, he made it clear she was not okay. "You should stay off it. I'll be gone for a few hours, and then we can figure out what's happening with the ferries and return to Seattle."

The remaining light left her eyes. "Cam, I'm not ready to talk about that yet."

He wasn't, either. The idea of leaving her, of walking away and letting some other man get to know her, made Cam want to rip Sandy's expensive house down stone by stone.

"I was thinking I could use a break and some time in Seattle. Thought you might have some ideas on how I could spend that time." Though if his hunch was right she was never going to want to see him again.

He pushed that thought away and concentrated on getting through the next hour and the assignment he'd given himself. He kissed her on the forehead. "I'll step out and be back."

"Let us know what's happening," Sandy said in his usual voice.

That wasn't going to happen, but it was time to plant as many seeds as possible. "Do I need to know anything for the alarm system to get back in?"

The older man didn't say anything. Didn't offer up a number or a detailed account of how to get around the system. Enough time passed that Julia noticed. She joined Cam in looking at Sandy while the answer came to him.

Julia glared at him. "Sandy?"

"I don't like giving it away," he said.

This guy had an obsession and Cam thought he knew why. "Understandable, but I don't like sleeping on the porch."

Sandy took a piece of paper out of one of the drawers and wrote a number on it. "Here."

Cam wasn't convinced whatever was written on that paper would do anything. But for Julia he would try. Try and hope he was wrong so they could avoid talking about this topic ever again.

A SHORT TIME later Cam pulled into the clinic's parking lot and went inside. There were people lined up against all the walls. The coughing echoed through the space until Cam was sure he'd come back out of the building with a disease.

He flashed his ID downstairs and then again on the assigned floor to get by the guards Connor had set up. After calling, Holt met him in the hall.

They walked side by side, but Holt started talking. "I thought you'd be in bed."

"I'm not tired. Too wound up." The exhaustion would hit him but it hadn't yet.

Holt chuckled. "I didn't mean sleeping."

Since the guy had handed him a box of condoms this last time, Cam knew Holt was on top of this subject. But Cam wasn't in the mood to talk about anything personal. "Is he talking?"

Holt didn't pretend not to understand. "No."

"I need him to."

"Yeah, well." Holt shrugged. "We all want that."

Looked as if he needed to spell this out a bit more. He was trying to remain vague in case they got questions. He didn't want trouble to roll over to Holt. "No, I need people to think he's talking. Naming names."

"Why?"

Damn, he was going to insist on details. That was probably fair, since for this to work Cam needed the assistance of the guards and some of the staff. "You know why."

Holt's eyes narrowed but a spark of understanding showed in his eyes. "You sure."

"I think so." The longer Cam thought about it the more clear the idea of Sandy being in the middle of this mess became.

Holt let out a low whistle. "This is a dangerous game for you."

Cam didn't care about the physical danger, but he knew that wasn't what Holt was talking about. He referred to how this could rip him and Julia apart. They'd had such a fragile relationship so far. The sex was great, but they both tiptoed around more and threw up trust concerns now and then.

Hell, Cam didn't know what he wanted with her or even what he could handle. He just knew that the idea of not seeing her after being in this intense relationship with her would crush something inside him. In a short time she had wrapped her life around his and he didn't know how to break them apart again…or if he even wanted to.

If he removed her, took her face and that body out of the equation, forgot all about her strength and the comfort in being with her and boiled her down to this person he was not connected to, the lingering question about Sandy would remain.

That meant he couldn't let this drop. Cam knew he had to dig and poke and risk her wrath. "But if I'm right about—"

Holt was already shaking his head. "You still lose because Julia is going to be furious. I was there when we delivered you guys to Sandy's house a short time ago. They have a connection." Cam had seen that, too. A pseudo father-daughter bond.

A genuineness of affection behind the gruff exterior. Still, Cam said, "Something is not right."

"Could you be jealous?" Holt said the words carefully, hesitating over each one.

The delivery didn't stop the rush of angry heat that breezed through Cam. "Julia isn't involved with the guy."

"I meant emotionally."

"That doesn't really sound like something I'd know about." But now he did. He got the idea of a connection. He'd experienced the sensation of having someone else's happiness mean more than anything—his needs, the job and everything else.

"You're not you when you're with her."

Cam knew exactly what his friend meant and dodged the comment. "It's only been a few days."

"It's about intensity, not actual time together."

"I know." But the words sounded weird coming from Holt. He was this big bruiser of a guy who had never had a serious girlfriend so long as Cam had known him. And here he was, talking about romance in a way that sounded like poetry.

Holt exhaled. "She's going to hate you."

"I know that, too." That was the part that kept stopping him even though he knew it was selfish. She needed him to do that right thing even when doing the wrong thing was too easy.

"Is this worth losing her? I can play the bad guy. If I'm wrong it won't matter." Leave it to Holt to offer.

But that was never going to work.

"If I can't live with myself, we don't have a future anyway." That was the closest Cam could get to admitting she might mean something. That if they made it through the fallout with Sandy, she might.

Holt made a hissing sound between his teeth. "You're stuck."

"Yeah, I know."

Chapter Nineteen

Julia sat curled up on the edge of the sofa in Sandy's impressive family room. The bed called to her, but she wanted to stay up until Cam got back. Something about the idea of snuggling under the covers with him sounded so good. After all they'd endured and survived, she wanted to touch him and kiss him and feel his heat. But he had to get back here first.

Sandy had gone into his home office over an hour ago. She hadn't heard a word since. She thought he'd come out and talk to her, maybe take her mind off everything. Even with Ray caught and Kreider gone, the path of destruction cut through Calapan was hard to ignore. Shattered lives and so many questions.

She got up and walked into the kitchen, thinking a second snack wouldn't be totally out of line. On the way in, the alarm panel in the dining room caught her attention. The red light beamed at her. If she was going to stay here a few days—and that was the plan in light of the questions she needed to answer—she needed to be able to come and go. That meant knowing the security codes. The one she had didn't work, which meant she didn't have access.

With her mind in a whirl she knew the chances of

her forgetting were pretty high. She decided to fix the problem now before she was standing out there one day in a rainstorm.

She dumped off the coffee mug and empty water bottle and made her way to the front door. She just wanted to double-check. The alarm pad was all lit up, but the only light that flashed was red. No green light here either, which made sense in light of a drug ring being run right under their noses.

Her feet padded against the hardwood as she went back to Sandy's office. She hated to disturb him, although Cam had raised a good question about Sandy not actually having any work right now.

Still, she was respectful. She held the knob in one hand as she knocked with the other. No one answered. Since she'd seen him go in an hour ago and since there was not a door in and out of there other than the main one into the hall, he had to be in there.

She looked at the knob and knocked again. She'd never burst into this room. She viewed this as his private space and didn't violate that sanctuary.

But something pulled hard at her tonight. She wanted to peek in and see what he did when he was alone and when he worked.

Inhaling a deep breath, she twisted the knob and pushed the door open. She saw the empty chair and the walls lined with bookshelves. But no Sandy. She tried to remember if she'd dozed off and maybe missed him. She doubted it.

She went to the house intercom system and called for him. Nothing there, either.

As she stood there she felt the walls close in. It was an odd sensation and not one based in reality, but she knew the red light meant no way out. She'd have to break a window or risk the alarm. The latter wouldn't be too bad except that the new system actually didn't let you accidentally set off the alarm. If the system was on and you didn't have the code, you were trapped in that room.

That suddenly seemed like a terrible idea. So did the thoughts going through her mind about Sandy's desk. It was right there. She could look through some of the paperwork, if only to let Cam know his initial suspicions were truly wrong.

And she might be able to clear up some of those questions about the shipyard's ownership. She couldn't believe Sandy didn't know. He was a man who knew everything down to the penny. But then, nothing had been normal about the past few days. They all wanted this episode over, except her, who wanted the part with Cam to linger.

She sat down in the oversize chair and was immediately transported back to being a kid. She'd sit in his chair and spin, pretending she was on an amusement park ride. She shifted the seat from side to side and opened the top drawer. The move felt so naughty she only got it out far enough to stare at the pens sitting in the tray.

That was enough. Snooping was not her style. If Cam needed proof or wanted to talk to Sandy, he could. She was not going to get in the middle of that.

She walked back to the alarm keypad by the front door. She entered the code and tried a few variations. By the fifth time she had the nerves in her belly jumping around in a chaotic frenzy.

People could talk about being comfortable at home and not wanting to leave. She got that. But being locked in made her twitchy. If Cam needed her, she couldn't get there…and that realization set something spinning inside her.

She went back into the family room and picked up the phone. Cam might jump to the wrong conclusions, but he might have a way to get out other than through an upstairs balcony. When she lifted the receiver she didn't hear anything on the other end. No dial tone. She hung up and tried again. Then another time.

By the time she slammed down the phone the last time, she was near frantic. She couldn't control her breathing or her thoughts. She started jumping to bigger conclusions than Cam had. Then she remembered her cell. She'd left it on the kitchen counter.

She raced back to the kitchen because plain walking no longer seemed fast enough. She stepped into the doorway and stopped. Sandy had cleaned off the counter after they ate, and the phone was gone.

She pulled open drawers and looked on every flat surface. She made a run in the bedroom to see if he'd thrown it on the bed. No luck.

She stood in the middle of the hall and thought it all through. No cell, no landline, no alarm code. No way out.

Maybe Cam wasn't so paranoid after all.

CAM TRIED JULIA'S cell for the third time. The phone rang and she didn't pick up. He wanted to write it off to her being tired and crawling into bed. Maybe she was so wiped out she'd turned off the sound.

There were a lot of reasonable possibilities. He kept dwelling on the awful, like that something had happened to her and she couldn't get to the phone.

The clinic floor was quiet, just as planned. They had the world thinking Ray was on the second floor. He was really on the third. They'd cleared patients out except for a few who couldn't or refused to be moved.

"What's wrong with you?" Holt came up beside him and leaned against the wall in the visitors' lounge.

Cam tried to keep the panic out of his voice. The anxiety whipping through him was enough to deal with. "I can't reach her."

Holt made a sound, something like a humph. "Maybe she needs a break."

"Didn't seem like it." If anything, she'd been trying to get him to commit to something. She'd been pretty unimpressed with his schedule and the danger aspects, probably because he was dragging her through the middle of danger at the time.

"Is your head in this?" Holt asked as he checked his watch.

"Yes."

Holt nodded and didn't say anything else on that topic. That was Holt's style. He didn't browbeat. He treated everyone like a grown-up, which was quite refreshing. That wasn't to say he didn't butt in, because he did. But had an innate sense of when to back down, and he used it now.

There was a broader principle at work. They had an understanding on the team: if you couldn't go for the job, for whatever reason, you spoke up. You did not put the other team members in danger. Cam knew the rule and lived by it. He spent almost every day with Holt and Shane. There was no way he was going to put them in a position of having to pick up for him.

And if he was right and Sandy presented a danger, then he needed to figure this out right now. The longer Julia spent in his house, trusting him while he did whatever he was doing, the worse the end could be. And one day he might decide that she knew too much or knew the wrong people, and then Cam didn't want to think what would happen.

But the worst part was they might get this close and not be able to finish this off. That was the line that Holt kept repeating, and he said a version of it here again. "He might not even show."

"He will." Cam knew that Holt, who was usually right about these things—about most things, except women—had this part wrong. Sandy's personality would not let him stay at home. If he thought he could fix this and save his reputation and all he'd built, he would. A guy who lived in that kind of house liked to send a personal message and would not be content to let that message flash about him being a drug dealer.

"Yeah, I think so, too." Holt looked down at his feet. "How are you going to explain that to her?"

Cam had run through the various options numerous times. It all came down to the same thing. He would have to pull her aside and tell her that the first man she'd ever trusted—one of the few she'd ever trusted—had violated that trust in a serious way. He had no idea how she'd recover from that.

So, for now, he dodged. "I can only handle one disaster at a time."

"That's not true, but I'll let you get away with that excuse."

THE CLINIC HALLWAYS were quiet except for the occasional squawk over the speakers. Emergencies requiring serious care were flown to Seattle. The clinic served all the other needs of the community. Tonight it also acted as the scene for a setup.

Cam stood in the bathroom of Ray's reported room. Back at the house Cam had made sure to give the information to Julia in an offhanded way and she'd repeated it in front of Sandy. Cam had witnessed that part.

With the silence coming from Sandy's house, Cam wanted to send Holt over, but they needed all three of them there. Cam went back and forth between wanting Sandy to show up and not. He believed to his bones the older man had some side business going on. One that wasn't legal. He'd love to be wrong, but he didn't think he was.

A long and painful hour passed with no signs of anything. The world outside the clinic had morphed into night and stretched into the early hours of the morning. The sky remained a dark gray, signaling another rainy day tomorrow.

Cam leaned his head back against the wall. He was about to call this off and check on Julia when he heard the footsteps. Not sneakers. These were dress shoes. If he guessed right, expensive black dress shoes that he'd already seen.

Whoever it was got by the guard, which was part of the plan. The guy was to sit there but get up for food and drinks. Set a pattern of not being great about being at the door. It didn't matter, since Ray wasn't on this floor. The real guard had strict orders, and after the way the guy got all wide-eyed and panic-stricken talking to Holt, Cam doubted that guard would mess up.

The footsteps grew louder and there was a muffled sound that Cam now associated with the door opening and closing. The sound of the privacy curtain being peeled back and the way the rings clanked against the bar suggested the guy was moving around. If he came into the bathroom he'd see cabinets and not Cam hiding inside. Out there he'd see a man with Ray's coloring sleeping on his stomach and all bandaged around the shoulder and stomach.

The Ray part was tougher to pull off. If Sandy bent down and looked in close, he'd see that the face smashed in the pillow did not belong to Ray. The hope was that he'd buy the room and the clinic and try to do the job fast.

Cam looked out of the crack in the door to the room beyond. Sandy walked around wearing doctor's scrubs. It was a nice but unnecessary touch. They'd already covered that with the guard. But now when nurses and other people on the hall ignored him, it wouldn't seem so odd.

Sandy slipped around the bed toward the headboard and the beeping equipment. Nothing was actually connected to Shane as he played Ray, but Sandy didn't need to know that. When Sandy took out a syringe and started filling the tubes he thought led into Ray, Cam felt sick. He didn't even know if Julia would believe him despite the other witnesses.

Cam slid out as Sandy finished. When he turned to leave he almost walked right into Cam.

Cam held his gun steady. "You're a doctor now?"

"I was… There was… Just checking on him." Sandy stumbled his way through a sentence that made no sense in light of who he was and his professed lack of knowledge about Ray Miner and who he was.

"Do you need him to come back to work at the drug-producing plant? Must be hard to find people loyal enough to do that." Cam almost spat. The guy made him sick.

Sandy was one of those. He had everything and greed pulled at him until he went out and earned more. And not the legal way. No, he had to move drugs. Cam would bet he was a guy who found drug use to be disgusting yet had no problem pushing it to kids and getting rich off them.

"What?"

Sandy was playing dumb and Cam refused to buy it. The blank stare and confusion. He was acting to the wrong audience. "It's over."

"I don't know what you think you have, but—"

Cam could almost see the wheels turning in the guy's head. He was searching for a reasonable explanation and kept coming up blank. Cam almost wished Sandy would come forward and admit it, not hide behind the money he earned from illegal drugs. Just own his behavior.

"You're a drug dealer and murderer." Cam had some other choice words for him but led with those two.

Sandy starting shaking his head. "You're passing your mess off on me."

"Why do this? Why drugs? I hear it's a huge operation with great stuff." Cam had promised he wouldn't ask, but the question came out.

He'd heard so many excuses and justifications over the years, most of them not true, that he no longer cared. The fact was, people committed these crimes and then acted shocked when caught. Sandy was the type to play the victim. Poor little millionaire got bored or was in the right place or whatever.

Cam worked his butt off in his job and paid the bills. He didn't expect a handout and he sure didn't understand people who had it all and threw it away in the search for *just a little bit more*.

Something came over Sandy. The fake fear in his eyes

faded. Now he looked tall and in charge and every bit the crime boss. "Moving the drugs is easy. Growing them is easy. And if you're really good and have the open land, it can be very lucrative." He smiled. "Or so I hear. I don't have personal experience, of course."

"Right." Cam was done playing this game. "Step away from the bed."

"Or I could shoot the person in here." Sandy brought out a gun that had been tucked into the waist of his pants. "Does this person mean anything to you? Actually, it doesn't matter, because you're one of those people who believes in others. Very tiresome."

Sandy brought the gun around and aimed it at the person in the bed.

Cam shook his head. "I wouldn't do that. He gets upset very easily."

"Why do I care?"

"Because he has a grenade." Cam said the code word for Shane to move.

He did not waste time. He brought his arm out from under him with the blade arcing through the air. Just as Sandy turned and aimed again, Shane stabbed his knife into Sandy's thigh.

The man dropped his gun and let it clank against the floor. He let out an awful scream, one that was almost inhuman in its piercing squeal. Then he bent over, holding the wound.

Real doctors came running and Holt slipped into the room. When Shane sat up, he looked down and watched Sandy make demands about his leg and a scar. After ripping the fake tubes out, he came to stand with Holt and Cam.

Sandy rocked back and forth on the floor while Holt

grabbed the discarded gun and a nurse tried to stop the bleeding. "You think you won, but I'll beat this."

The guy fought to the end. Cam guessed a part of him should admire that, but it was hard to after hearing that squeal. "Good luck wasting your money doing that."

Sandy's head whipped up and he pinned Cam with an intense stare. "And in the meantime you lose Julia."

"She loves you." Cam wasn't clear why at the moment. "Why would you do this to her?"

Sandy's rage spilled out of him now. There was nothing fatherly or caring about the guy huddled on the floor in a sitting position. "I am convenient to her. I did everything for her and she left. She was as useless as her father and look what happened to him."

Cam remembered the story. "He fell."

"Fell. Sure." Sandy laughed.

Everything inside Cam went cold. He heard Holt swear under his breath and saw Shane take a step back while he shook his head. "You're saying that you—"

"You might want to get to my house." Sandy clenched his teeth as the nurse continued to work on his leg. "No phone. No way out. Julia could be on the edge right now."

Cam imagined her trying to get out of the house. All frantic and confused and winding up. "Why would you do that?"

"Because for once I needed her to listen and do what she was told."

The comment was so cold, so awful, that Cam knew he couldn't repeat it. Sandy had belittled her and expressed disappointment. And unless Cam misheard, Sandy had also admitted to doing something to Julia's drunken father.

"So you hate women," Shane said.

Sandy scoffed. "I hate weakness, and she and her father are all about weakness."

"That's where you're wrong." Right there was where Cam wrote the guy off. He couldn't speak to Julia's father, but he did know all about her. "She's stronger than both of us."

Chapter Twenty

Julia couldn't take the confinement one more second. She stood at the bank of glass doors that ran along the back of the house and stared into the lit yard beyond. The security lights plunged the patio and pool into a burst of white. She wasn't much of a swimmer, but right now she wanted to run out there and jump in. Cold or not, didn't matter.

Her insides jumped and tingled. Every nerve seemed to be on fire or ready to burst. She'd never thought of herself as nervous or anxious, but being locked in, penned against her will and unable to contact anyone, had her walking around and dreaming up crazy ways to get out.

She'd paced so much she'd broken out in a sweat. The landline phone lay on the floor. No dial tone. A laptop was open and the television was on. Nothing got her access to the world beyond the walls. It didn't even matter that these were pretty well-decorated walls. Prison was prison.

Her footsteps thundered as she ran up to Sandy's bedroom again. She'd made this journey twice already. She'd seen how Cam got them out. Just tie the sheets and jump. But without him here she didn't trust herself to go. She did trust Cam.

He'd been right about Sandy. She didn't know what

was going on, but what was happening now was so odd. She couldn't wrap her brain around it. Didn't believe she'd be okay without him.

She heard a pounding. At first she thought it was wishful thinking or her brain playing tricks. Then the doorbell began to ring. Over and over. Chiming until she felt it inside her head.

She ran downstairs, looking first at the front door. As soon as she appeared in the small window next to the double door, Shane waved and pointed toward the back of the house.

She should have been angry, but all she felt was relief. It almost knocked the legs out from under her. She spun around on her heel and got to the glass doors again. Holt and Cam stood out there, looking as if they were locked in deep thought. Holt held a gun but Cam shook his head.

Cam glanced up and smiled. A warmth filled her when she saw that face. He was fine and here and everything would be okay. Even if she never got out of this house again.

"The alarm is in shutdown." She yelled the words because she knew the glass would muffle them.

For some reason he seemed to know. He nodded and bent down. When he stood up again he had a planter in his arms, and not a small one. This thing could break glass and bones.

The first hit bounced off the glass, but her belief never wavered. He might talk about not caring about a woman and keeping things light, but that look of determination did not say acquaintance to her. The second hit landed square against the glass and a huge cracking sound split the night. She waited for the glass to fall. He stood on the other side looking as if he was trying to will it to fall.

Finally he motioned her back and lifted his leg. As Holt yelled something, Cam kicked. The glass exploded. It shattered into pieces, breaking off into slivers as it crashed over the dining room table and pinged in what looked like a million tiny cubes against the hardwood floor.

Then he was there. He had her wrapped in his arms and was kissing her hair. He said something about trust, but she didn't hear it. Couldn't hear anything over the frantic beating of her heart.

The night was a blur, but he was solid. She ran her hands over him and tugged him in close. Her last thought was relief.

Then the world went dark.

CAM SAT BY Julia's bedside at the clinic and willed her to wake up. The doctor had chalked her reaction up to anxiety and shock. Cam didn't like either answer. Also hated that she still hadn't opened her eyes.

He put her hand between both of his and rubbed. The heat had slowly returned to her body. When she first passed out she'd felt like ice. Her skin had actually been cold to the touch.

"How are we doing?" Holt asked as he opened the door and came in.

Shane followed. "Looks like she's not ready to wake up yet."

The doctor had said the same thing. Cam now hated that phrase.

He glanced at her, saw her hair on the white pillow and the slow rise and fall of her chest. "Apparently."

Shane walked around the bed, looking at her. Whatever he was looking for he must have found, because he stopped at the end of her bed and stood there. "What are you going to tell her when she wakes up?"

Cam had walked through that in his mind. Over and over. He could soft-pedal it all and fill in blanks. But that wouldn't be fair. She'd been strong and right by his side throughout the entire ordeal. He owed her as much information as he could give her and a shoulder to cry on when the disappointment about Sandy hit.

"The truth." He'd mess up if he tried to do anything else, anyway.

"Smart." Holt nodded. "But that's a rough story. Her uncle—"

"They weren't blood related." For some reason, that mattered to Cam. He didn't want her tied to Sandy any more than she was.

"I don't think that will be a comfort, since he ran drugs, killed, scared her on purpose, tried to kill you and possibly killed her father."

Man, that list. Cam ran through it in his head, but hearing it out loud sounded so much worse. And that wasn't even all of it. He knew it would get worse over the next few days as they gathered more information on the choices Sandy had made. Then came the criminal part. No way would that man go down easy.

But that wasn't even the biggest problem of all. Julia's feelings for him were. "She loved him."

Shane snorted. "Well, her taste in men stinks."

"Thanks." Since that actually made Cam smile, he didn't bother to shoot an insult right back at his teammate.

Holt looked over at him. "I guess this means you're off the market."

"Was I ever on it?" Cam kept his dating life light. It had been a good system until he met Julia.

"You were single." Holt shrugged as a smile tugged at the corner of his mouth. "Fight it all you want, but I saw the look on your face. You want her."

The knee-jerk reaction to deny and minimize had faded. When Holt delivered his assessment, Cam could only agree. "I do."

Shane put a hand on Cam's shoulder. "Then don't mess it up."

That seemed simple enough. Maybe too simple. "That's your advice?"

"Hey, it's good advice." Shane walked toward the door.

"Call us if you need a ride," Holt said as he joined Shane. "Otherwise, Connor said you should take some time off."

"He's a hopeless romantic." Cam had never thought he'd say that about a six-foot-something bruiser who could shoot and run and do anything Corcoran needed. But Cam did admire Connor's ability to balance his marriage and the work. He wasn't the only one. The entire Annapolis office was paired off.

They'd all survived dating. Maybe he could, too. He rubbed a thumb over the back of Julia's hand. Maybe it just depended on the partner.

"I'm thinking all of you have marriage fever." Holt sounded disgusted by the possibility.

Shane touched his chest. "Except me."

Holt nodded. "Right, except me and Shane."

Cam remembered saying something similar and thinking it was brilliant. Now he knew better. "Your time will come."

Holt's smile fell. "Don't come back with that attitude."

JULIA CAME AWAKE in bursts. She'd wake up and try to open her eyes, then drift again. Every time she thought she'd reached the surface, she would feel a hand in hers or the brush of fingers through her hair. It was that loving touch that had her keep trying. She craved it.

On the last swim to the top she heard her name spoken in a deep, husky voice. She knew that voice, which meant she knew that hand. Using all her energy, she opened her eyes. The light flooded in and had her blinking. She wanted to lift her hand to block it, but her muscles weighed too much to lift.

"Hey there." Cam leaned in farther as she woke up.

"What happened?" She remembered being in the house and the sense of desperation. Then there was glass everywhere. She didn't even know what had happened to Sandy and why he'd locked the house down.

"Sandy set the security system and you couldn't get out." Cam kept up the gentle caress of his fingertips against the back of her hand. "The doctor said that shock along with being dehydrated was too much for your system."

"Am I okay?"

"Yes." He leaned down and kissed her forehead. "You need rest, which is what I think I said to you about a hundred times."

She wanted to roll her eyes, but it hurt to move her head. "I'm not weak."

"Of course not." His head pulled back. "Is that what you thought I was saying?"

She thought back to all he'd told her. He'd praised her. She didn't remember the word *weak* or any other negative word. He wasn't her father or like any man she'd ever dated. "I just wanted you to know."

He raised their joined hands to his mouth and kissed her fingers. "I know."

She knew she should close her eyes and drift off. Him being there made her feel safe, but there were so many questions spinning in her head. She started with the obvious one. "Sandy was involved, wasn't he?"

A flash of pain crossed over Cam's face. She knew then that he was trying to hold that back and protect her. But she'd already guessed the truth. The second she'd looked for her cell and found it gone and then couldn't get out of the house, her mind had gone from thinking Sandy was being overprotective to knowing he was hiding something.

Part of her wanted to believe he'd done it because he hadn't thought Cam safe. But she knew that wasn't it. Sandy had become secretive, and that security system kept growing to include new and scary features. When she'd stopped visiting, his mood had turned surly.

Cam continued to hold her hand in his. "We think Sandy is the drug runner, Julia. The boss. In charge of it all."

She closed her eyes and tried to let those words sink in. "I can't imagine him doing it."

She'd never known him to use drugs or even alcohol. He'd shamed her father repeatedly on the alcohol issue. It made her wonder if dealing was his way of proving he was stronger and everyone else was weaker. That did fit with his personality.

"He pretty much admitted it to me and the team." Cam exhaled. "He got caught up in telling us how great he was and started talking about this."

"I bet he's trying to back off of that admission now." The thought of Sandy in prison made her mind rebel. The guy liked comfort. Big-time comfort. Thinking about him in a uniform with set mealtimes... What had he been thinking?

"We set him up at the hospital and he took the bait. Came to the clinic to kill Ray, the one guy who could finger him, but it was really Shane in the bed."

The body blows kept coming. That was not the man she knew. Watching who he was unwind in front of her made her wonder if she knew anything about men.

She glanced up at the only other man who had meant so much to her. She lay there waiting for Cam to deliver the news that he was off to a new assignment or going to live under a new name. There was an automatic finality that came with being with him.

"You can just tell me." She braced for the pain that would come when he uttered the words. "You don't have to be careful with your words or worry about my feelings."

Instead, he frowned at her. "What?"

"That you're leaving. How you hate commitment."

"When did I say that?"

"You've said it before and I want you to know I'm ready for the speech." But she wasn't. She totally wasn't.

"Do you want me to go?" He laid her hand against the bed but kept his over it.

"No." She practically screamed the answer. A nurse walking by in the hallway did a double take.

He shot her that sexy dimpled smile. "Then why are you trying to get me to say something I don't want to say?"

Her brain kept misfiring. She had no idea what they were talking about or how they'd gotten here from where they were the last time they'd discussed this subject. "But you—"

"Julia, I wasn't kidding when I told you I felt something I'd never felt before. I haven't had wild love affairs or had the benefit of growing up in a big family and watching my siblings pair off." He switched seats so that he sat on the edge of her bed. "I want you."

"A date." It felt risky to even put that out there knowing how he felt about the subject.

"I'm hoping for a lot of dates." His eyes gleamed. "See, I'm falling for you and it seems to me when that happens, two people should spend a lot of time together."

She couldn't figure out how to open her mouth to speak.

"Let's try this." He lowered his head and took her mouth with his. The dragging kiss had her remembering every touch and wanting so many more.

When he lifted his head again, her body sparked to life. This time she grabbed his hand and pressed it right between her breasts. "That falling thing?"

"Yeah?"

Oh, that smile. "You're not falling alone."

Falling, fell. They could use whatever words he wanted. She just knew she thought about him all the time, even when he was right beside her. Something about him—the charm or maybe the bossiness—had gotten under her skin from the beginning.

He turned his hand to trace a line along her collarbone. "In the interests of disclosure, my world is about danger and secrets and—"

"I've known that from day one. Literally." He'd busted into the house and nothing had ever been the same.

"True." His expression grew serious. "I want to give us a chance. A real chance."

She was in for that. She could give him as long as he needed. She'd waited. "So long as we give it a nice long chance."

He nuzzled her nose with his. "Months and months."

She grabbed his face and held it in front of her. "No more informal dating."

He gave her a quick kiss on the cheek. "Not with you."

"I knew I liked you from the beginning." She wrapped her arms around his neck and brought him in closer.

His laugh had someone outside the door hesitating for a second. The person stood there and then moved on.

"Now be honest," he said with a smile. "You didn't like me all that much for a long while."

That was probably fair. The beginning part, anyway. The fear had come first and quickly dissipated. The driving need and blinding attraction had seemed to settle in and refuse to go, even after they'd slept together. "But the second I got to know you, I was hooked."

He leaned down, almost climbed into bed with her. "And I plan to keep you that way."

She rubbed her hand up his arm. "I like your style, Cameron Roth."

"And I like everything about you, Julia White."

"Then let's get me out of here and to that hotel you promised."

He winked at her. "Done."

Chapter Twenty-One

Holt and Shane sat down in the bar nearest to the clinic. Watching Cam fall deserved a beer. Maybe a bottle of gin. The good thing about this island was they had plenty of those. Seemed something about the cool, wet air got people drinking.

Law enforcement had swooped in and started investigating everything. It looked as though Sandy was in big trouble going forward. Ray hadn't rolled, but Shane and Holt had a bet he would.

Neither Ray nor Sandy was the type to thrive in prison. They both had skills, but their egos were problematic. The prosecutor was already offering a deal for testimony. Ray would be dumb not to take it.

Shane lifted his beer in salute. "We lost another one."

"And Cam." Holt felt he should say a prayer or something. "He was pretty clear that he was out when it came to the long-term-girlfriend thing."

"That vow lasted all of four seconds after he met Julia."

"She is hot." Holt had to be fair about that. She was off-the-charts pretty and probably way out of Cam's league, or at least that was what Holt planned to tell him all the time.

"And she didn't spook when guys died in front of her. She held on." Shane nodded. "Yeah, you're right. She is hot."

"It's like a disease in the office." Holt touched his chest because the idea of hooking up and getting married gave him pain. "Any chance there's a vaccine?"

"I'd ask, but then I'd accidentally insult one of them."

Made sense, since the *entire* office was now taken except for him and Shane. Connor and his wife had been estranged, but the rest of them had found women and in record time went from confirmed bachelors making fun of the married agents to one of them. The traveling team had vowed to stay out of the fray, but now that deal was busted, as well.

Shane lifted his half-empty glass. "I'm going to need another one."

"What if Ms. Right is here tonight?" Holt looked around, scanned one table after the other. But he never saw what the others did. He got pretty. He liked smart and resourceful.

"If the right woman comes in, I'll know because she'll buy me a beer." Shane stared at the door. When it remained closed and he didn't have a new beer in front of him, he shrugged.

That was the Shane Holt loved and admired. "Romantic."

"We need a new pact," Shane said. "Except..."

Holt knew this was going to be bad. "What?"

"I bet you're next."

"Double or nothing." Holt was willing to hand over his house to win that one.

"We'll see." Shane downed the last of the glass. "We'll see."

* * * * *

*Look for SHELTERED, the next book
in HelenKay Dimon's* CORCORAN TEAM:
BULLETPROOF BACHELORS *miniseries,
next month. You'll find it wherever
Harlequin Intrigue books and ebooks are sold!*